HANNAH EDWARDS
SECRETS OF RIVERWAY

HANNAH EDWARDS
SECRETS OF RIVERWAY

Ashley Hards

Fabled Films Press
New York

Copyright © 2024 by Fabled Films LLC

All rights reserved. No part of this book may be used or reproduced in any manner whatsoever without written permission from the publisher except in the case of brief quotations embodied in critical articles or reviews. For information address Fabled Films LLC, 200 Park Avenue South, New York, NY 10003.
info@fabledfilms.com

Published by Fabled Films LLC, New York

ISBN: 978-1-944020-91-0
Library of Congress Control Number: 2023949116

First Edition: September 2024

Cover Designed by Jaime Mendola-Hobbie
Jacket Art by Bev Johnson & Jaime Mendola-Hobbie
Interior Book Design by Lauren Woodrow
Text Set in P22 Mackinac Pro, Zilla Slab, and KG Love Ya Like A Sister
Printed by Everbest in China

FABLED FILMS PRESS
NEW YORK CITY

fabledfilms.com

For information on bulk purchases for promotional use, please contact Fabled Films Press Sales department at info@fabledfilms.com

For Oscar,
who I will always wear in my heart of heart.

1
SOMETHING IS
ROTTEN
IN RIVERWAY

Are you looking for a place where the fun flows as fast as a mountain river? A place that is best described as *cute*, *quaint*, and *cozy*? If so, and you're near Riverway, I recommend that you drive right through it. Don't stop. Don't even slow down.

A few months ago, someone went missing from Riverway. Just vanished. So trust me, you'll want to keep going.

Oh—you think that's a reason to stop? You like a good mystery?

Let me tell you some more about the town. Then I bet you'll change your mind.

Like most tourists, you'll find Riverway by driving south on Highway 1. Highway 1 weaves through seas of never-ending canola fields. The canola plants' seeds are used to make vegetable oil, and you'll find their yellow flowers cheery and cheesy—like boxed macaroni.

At first, you'll be happy you've left the dull fields of wheat behind. But soon the canola-yellow will become monotonous. You will wonder: Is there ever going to be an end to this obnoxious yellow? Is it right to use this much space for a single crop? Just how much cooking oil does a country need?

Then, just when you start dreaming about painting the canola any color but yellow, a rusted barbed wire fence will mark the end of the field. Behind it will be acres of dry, yellowing grass. This grass is a natural part of the prairie. It doesn't stand stiff like canola. It shifts pleasantly like fur in the wind.

Off in the distance, you'll see a wooden sign—the touristy type that makes the ideal background for a group photo:

RIVERWAY
THE TOWN WHERE THE RIVER FLOWS
POP. 2000

Behind this sign is a large canyon, where—one would presume—the river is flowing. Many a tourist will pull over to the side of the highway, hoping for a phenomenal view of a river carving its way into the prairie ground. They are consistently disappointed. Riverway would be better dubbed: "The Town Where the River *Used* to Flow." What was once a raging river is now a trickling stream.

Okay, let's say you have no choice. Maybe you're low on gas, or really hungry, or you've been driving for hours and need a bathroom. So you decide to stop in Riverway. Well . . . you're going to find it's just as disappointing as the river.

Riverway's downtown is split by Highway 2A East and Highway 2A West. On either side is a town that looks like a deserted cowboy movie set. There are two gas stations and two diner-style restaurants, one on each side, a strip of various (two) antique stores, a bookstore, a pharmacy, a small bank, a candy store, and an abandoned grain mill. (Insider's tip: The best dinner you can buy is in the gas stations.)

The townsfolk are proud of maintaining this fake Western charm. Most of the stores double as people's houses, and there is no clear division between where a shop ends and a house begins. One angry review of Jemma's Gems: Rare Antiques and Toys complains:

> Two stars. Interesting shop but terrible service. Picked up what looked like a vintage teacup only to realize that it was filled with coffee. The owner (I presume Jemma) accused me of tampering with her drink and chased me out of the shop! Went next door to Joe's Antique Emporium.

This, I assure you, is the usual experience in our shops. They aren't set up for browsing. For instance, if you want something from Jemma, she will search through four different drawers, peer under cabinets, and eventually find it underneath a couch cushion. Joe is a bit more professional: He never loses anything in the couch.

After stopping at a diner for a quick hamburger, most people get back in their cars and say, "I can't imagine how anybody lives here!" then quickly leave. But if you were to make the terrible mistake and stay, you might wander into Riverway's *booming* residential neighborhood. Which is the first left after the Sweets Shoppe, about five hundred yards away.

The residential area is like any other suburb, except the lawns are more yellow than green. The lucky people live near the Dustin Murkle Memorial Park, which includes a baseball diamond, bleachers, two swing sets, one set of monkey bars, a balance beam (all rusted), and a fountain, complete with the statue of evil Wallace "Big Gun" Morrow. Wallace is the town's not-so-famous Wild West villain.

But most people, the unlucky people, live in bungalows on Creekside Avenue, surrounded by hundreds of other bungalows with yellowing lawns. And the unluckier people (like me) live on Riverlane Way. Our houses were supposed to be on prized waterfront property, not the dusty riverbed view we have now.

There's a winding gravel path that makes up the Riverway Walk: An Attraction for All Ages. This gravel path twists and turns through the gulch, crossing over the river and circling back along the highway. It is also the site of Riverway Elementary School's Annual First-Grade Nature Walk—a field trip that is almost as disappointing as this town.

Riverway Preschool is right beside Riverway High School. It's a short, brown brick building that could be easily mistaken for a jail. Riverway High School is made of gray concrete. Its old windows let in rain, snow, wind, and whatever insects are in season. It is three stories tall—the tallest building in Riverway. And because of its size, it's not "just" a high school—it is an elementary and middle school as well.

There has to be more to this town than this, you think. So you wander into the Riverway Tourist Center. Attached to the pharmacy, this small booth houses a tour guide from 3:00 p.m. to 4:15 p.m. every other Tuesday. But if the guide is on a coffee break (and they usually are), just look for Rick. He's the "sheriff" for the volunteer police department and our local history buff, and you can ask him anything about the town! He will tell you how the river once made it a bustling center for trade—trade that attracted infamous cowboys like Wallace "Big Gun"

Morrow, who disappeared without a trace, leaving his hidden treasure behind.

And, finally, we do have a "local heritage site." It's the Old Grain Mill. It was built when everyone around here grew barley. But years later, canola became popular. So the farmers turned away from grain, and the mill shut down. It was scheduled for demolition eight different times, but the townspeople saved it.

As the river slowed (the townsfolk never say "dried up"), some of the surrounding farms turned to ranching. But many continued to grow canola. They worked for the famous Canola King.

Some people think Riverway feels like a ghost town. But I think it's more like a zombie town. The people go about their daily lives, staring blankly a good deal of the time, rarely questioning events, big or small. I got proof of that four months ago, at the start of that mystery I told you about. That's when my father, the famous Canola King, disappeared.

2
THE "SEARCH" FOR THE CANOLA KING

My father was basically the soul of this town, which meant that he was always busy. But no matter how much work he had, he always made time to meet me down at the riverbank a few days a week after school. We played all sorts of games—from frog catching, to rock skipping, to even pretending to be pirates. Okay, playing pirates was when I was five. I'm eleven now, so we haven't done that in a while.

Anyway, I knew something was wrong the day he didn't show up. I waited for a while, staring at groups of minnows making circles in the shallow water, sighting the occasional weird diving-bug thing and making a note to ask Dad what it was.

After about an hour, I walked home. I arrived in time to see Rick's car parked in front of the house. He was standing on the doorstep, hands on his hips, hat over his chest, nodding as my mom spoke to him. When she saw me, she rushed toward me, asking if I'd seen Dad. She'd been looking for and couldn't find him.

We spent the following half hour listening to Rick talk about "the next steps."

In a big city, my dad's disappearance might not have seemed unusual. I imagine some burnt-out detective there saying people go missing all the time. Maybe I had too much faith in small-town living, but I expected more from Riverway. I'd imagined endless rows of police cars from the surrounding towns flooding Main Street, and lots of yellow **DO NOT CROSS** tape, and people dusting for fingerprints on random items in my dad's study. Most important, I'd imagined specially trained dogs roaming the canola fields to pick up my father's scent. And one dog (about five days into the search)—Hero—would raise his snout, sniff the air, then howl. "Hero, do you have something? Go get him!" Richard (Hero's faithful handler) would say, and Hero would run toward a hill and find my dad.

In my imagination, my dad would have tripped on a root and broken his ankle, but aside from being hungry and cold, he would mostly be all right. When we were reunited in a big bear hug, Dad would swear that he'd never ever leave Mom and me alone again. A single tear would fall down his cheek. Roll credits.

Needless to say, I was expecting more than Rick and

two volunteer deputies showing up the next day to nod some more and take notes. I was expecting more than a three-day "around the clock, but only in the mornings" search conducted by the local townsfolk. I was expecting more from the county police's "special task force," whose special task was hanging hundreds of **MISSING PERSON** posters around town. (Posters that have since turned yellow and tattered.)

I guess that was a lot for a zombie town, but it wasn't enough for me.

Sure, there are Rick's weekly check-ins, when he tells us "We are still hot on the case—don't you worry" and pats my mom on the shoulder. And there is a constant stream of people offering us mushy casseroles and assuring us "If there's anything, *anything*, we can do, please let us know."

But it's been four months since my dad's disappearance, and the trail of casseroles is finally starting to subside. And Rick is sounding less and less confident. Everyone is slowly losing interest, except Uncle Fergus, my dad's brother.

Mom says that we should be grateful for Uncle Fergus, that he misses Dad, too, and that he's really taken the pressure off her by managing the farm while Dad's away. But unlike the other casserole bringers, Uncle Fergus doesn't know when to stop. He lurks in the house for hours, "helpfully" volunteering to do the dishes and later shoving a sponge in my hand, saying back in his day, the kids would always volunteer to clean up. He's always offering important tips: Go to bed earlier and you'll be less tired. Hold your toothbrush at a forty-five degree angle and you'll brush better. Watch TV with a light on so you don't ruin your eyes.

Most grown-ups seem to see all this as friendly advice, but I know what he's really doing. He's trying to control us. And trying to convince us that *he* knows us better than we know ourselves. Listening to Uncle Fergus too much will dissolve your brain. Make you into a robot. A zombie. He has to be stopped.

My mom does not support my efforts to prevent a Fergus zombie apocalypse. Take, for example, Uncle Fergus's visit tonight. As always, he showed up unannounced and *insisted* on cooking us a "homemade meal." After hours of clanging pots and pans, he ushered us into the dining room, proudly placing plates before us.

"Please, go ahead, eat it before it gets cold! I learned this recipe during my exploration of Italy." Fergus then launched into a five-minute monologue about the Italy trip. A story we've heard enough times that I've basically memorized it.

As he rambled, I poked at the pasta, which had a particularly slippery quality, suspiciously like canned pasta.

I placed a limp noodle in my mouth—and was hit by a familiar taste: Chef Spaghettini's Quality Italian Bolognese.

"Well, Hannah, what do you think?" I looked up from the gloppy tomato concoction to see Uncle Fergus's expectant grin—the one he has when he's not asking you what you really think but wanting you to shower him with compliments.

"It's good," I said. Which wasn't a lie—I always looked forward to Mom packing Chef Spaghettini's pasta in my lunch bag.

"Good how?" Fergus prodded.

I'd love to say that I don't know what came over me—that I don't know why I said what I said next—but that wouldn't be true. I was tired of having Uncle Fergus tell me what's good for me. Popping by without any warning. Cooking us "food" and sitting in my dad's seat—as if he was pretending to be my dad. So I told him the truth. "Your pasta tastes exactly like Chef Spaghettini's. Did you learn how to make it from him when you were in Italy?"

"Excuse me, young lady—" Uncle Fergus began, preparing to launch into one of his zombie lectures, but my mom (mercifully) cut him off. "Fergus, I apologize for Hannah's behavior. Hannah, that was uncalled for. Go to your room."

Three hours later, I heard the front door close and Uncle Fergus's sports car drive away. Then Mom knocked on my door. She entered carrying two objects: a plate of

Jemma's sweet potato casserole (the most edible of the bunch) and a small leather-bound journal.

"I thought you'd be hungry." She gestured toward the food. "And that you might want a place to write things down—instead of saying them to Uncle Fergus and hurting his feelings. It'll help you process . . . everything."

As she said "everything," her eyes got just a little bit shinier. Mom had given up on finding Dad. I don't know if she thought he'd left us and wasn't coming back. Or if something terrible had happened to him and he couldn't come back. And I didn't ask her about it because I needed to believe he was going to show up with a logical explanation and everything would go back to normal.

Anyway, "I didn't mean to hurt anybody's feelings" is what I should have said. "Thank you, Mom" is another thing I should have said. Instead, I rolled my eyes. "Good night, Mom" is what I actually said.

I love my mom, but the truth is I've always been closer to my dad. Mom is great when you have a job to do—like making cookies or working on a tough homework assignment. Dad has always been more spontaneous. That's not to say that my mom isn't fun—she tells me very cool stories about when she was a kid. I just feel like she has to really work at getting to know me, whereas Dad just gets things without trying. Ever since Dad has been gone, those attempts to "get to know me" now feel like a full-on invasion. When I come home, she's always asking, "How was your day?" and "Are you feeling all right?" and "Do you have any plans?" I guess she's trying to be nice, but sometimes I don't want to think about if I am okay or not. This journal was just another piece of the "Are you okay?" puzzle.

Once she left, I opened it. My mom had written, "Hannah's Grief Journal. Lots of Love, Mom" on the first page. I ripped it out and threw the journal on the floor. The *last* thing I wanted to do was write down my thoughts. After my fit, however, I felt bad about beating up the journal.

Some people might say that believing objects have feelings is a little kid thing, but I don't think about it that way. Imagine: What if this journal had been sitting on the bookshelf for weeks, dreaming what it could be? Maybe it thought its owner would be an author, or a poet, or maybe the journal envisioned it would become a diary or a sketchbook. The journal was probably eagerly mulling over these possibilities when my mom picked it off the shelf and put it in her tote bag. When it was handed to me, it probably hoped that I would jump for joy and open my heart, excited to spill its contents onto the pages. No part of the journal would have ever suspected that I would be mean, especially since the journal did nothing wrong.

Holding back tears, I picked up the journal, grabbed some tape, and carefully replaced the first page. Then I took a black pen and wrote "Property of Hannah Edwards" below my mother's inscription. Once the ink had dried, I tenderly turned to the first page to "process" what was going on.

And this was my first entry:

> Journal, "What is going on?" you might ask. Well, what is going on is that the school year is about to start, my dad has been missing for 120 days, and I can't eat another bite of casserole. There's only one solution: From this day forth, I vow to use this journal not to process "things," but to mark my progress on my new case. I am going to solve the disappearance of the Canola King. And I'm not going to let anyone, not even Fergus, stop me.

So . . . that's everything you need to know about this town. And more than I meant to tell you about my father's disappearance. Do you still plan on sticking around? Well, that's up to you. But, really, you must have better things to do.

3
SCHOOL
OR AS I LIKE TO CALL IT: BEING TRAPPED IN A NUTSHELL

> WARNING!
>
> STOP RIGHT NOW.
>
> TRESPASSER, THIS IS MY JOURNAL, AND IF YOU'RE READING IT, YOU'D BETTER HAVE MY PERMISSION. AND IF YOU HAVE MY PERMISSION, YOU'D BETTER KEEP ALL THIS CONFIDENTIAL! OR ELSE . . .

Dear Journal,

In Ms. Luna's class today, we were learning about the different kinds of sentences and where to add commas. This sentence is called a simple sentence. There are lots of types of sentences. Another one is the compound sentence. That's a pretty easy one to make. Just add *and*, *but*, or *or* and a comma to connect two sentences instead of separating them with a period, but somehow nobody else in Ms. Luna's class gets that. (Haha! That last sentence I wrote is a compound sentence.)

It's hard to describe exactly what it's like for me to sit in class. Just imagine that every class—no matter how new—feels like it has been repeated a million times. And the teacher—no matter what—is speaking too slowly. You know you should pay attention because *technically* you haven't learned this before, but no amount of concentration or active listening or note-taking can make you focus. So you let your hand robotically move across the page, writing whatever the teacher is saying, but the words are just scratching the surface of your head. They aren't being absorbed into your brain. What's going on in your brain? Why does it feel like it's being stabbed by the shrill whining of the classroom's ancient fluorescent lights? How does nobody else hear this? Have you always heard this—did you just ignore it, drown it out up until now? How can you sit still when you want to escape the lights and the slow speaking and the repetitive material because, after all, there are bigger things to do—more urgent things—and if they are not done RIGHT NOW, then they may never get done?

But you don't want to leave class because then you

would be a *BAD KID,* and that would probably cause the world to explode. Because if you're usually a *GOOD KID* and you've gone and done something they think is bad, there's all this worry that you're becoming a *BAD KID.* And they'll treat you like you are a carrier of the plague or, as teachers say, "a disappointment."

Next, they will call your parents and warn them that you were acting like a *BAD KID,* and if you aren't careful, you'll become a *problem child.* A problem child is a kid so infected with *badness,* they are beyond saving. There is no cure for being a problem child. Teachers will dismiss you, other kids will avoid you, and your future boss will never trust you (or so they say).

Becoming the problem child must be avoided at all costs. It is a label you can never shake off—a permanent disfigurement, a scar on your soul that says, "This person is trouble, and they will always be trouble." Therefore, no matter how boring the class, no matter how unbearable it is to sit still, no matter how glaring the lights, I always try to pretend to be a *GOOD KID.*

I've never told anyone about my problem. Not Mom. Not Dad. Not anyone. I need to keep it a secret. I don't want anyone to think I'm a *BAD KID,* and I don't want the kids in school to think I'm weird. And I'm doing a good job hiding all of this. After all, as far as Ms. Luna can tell, I am actively listening.

To prove my point: This is what happened today when she called on me.

"Tim, good try, but that's not quite right. Hannah? Can you answer the question?" I didn't hear the question, but I couldn't say that because Ms. Luna thinks I *always* hear the question.

"Can you rephrase the question, Ms. Luna?" (Great move—she will never know!)

"Absolutely. I was just asking the class where to put a semicolon in a sentence."

I quickly glanced down at my notes. "Well, a semicolon is used in a compound sentence as a replacement for the comma and the word *and*."

Mary turned around and gave me a dirty look. We've been in an unspoken competition since she moved here in second grade. It's clear that she was the teacher's favorite at her old school, and she resents my reputation as the smart kid. Even though I find her to be a bit annoying, I like the way she beads her box braids. She uses only silver and gold beads, and they shimmer when she moves her head. They also clack together, which isn't great because I find that kind of distracting. And I really admire her perfect color-coded notes. I used to make notes like that. Lately, mine are covered in barely legible writing and a lot of bird drawings. Color-coding is what you do when you really care about the material—when you need to try hard to remember it. Now the material glides through my brain—it's just not worth the extra effort. Besides, I have bigger things on my mind. Like, you know, the whole "missing father" thing that everyone seems to have forgotten about.

"Great job as usual, Hannah!" Ms. Luna gave me an encouraging nod and turned back to the whiteboard, placing a semicolon where I had suggested. These things happen all the time. I am not paying attention, but nobody can really tell. It's very stressful, covering up all the time, pretending everything is okay.

Journal, at this point you might be wondering why I'm writing all this here since I promised I was going to use you for my investigation into my dad's disappearance. Well, that's exactly what I'm doing, because my investigation started at this moment in this classroom—when my friend Sam Castillo passed me an unbelievable note.

"Psst. Hannah. Hannah. Hannah." Sam poked me with his pencil. Sam is my best friend on the entire planet and a rare phenomenon: a quiet jock. He's got two older sisters, and they introduce him to their friends, so it feels like the whole school knows who he is. I wouldn't say that he's popular, but everybody likes him. I mean, who wouldn't like a guy who will teach you to throw better instead of making fun of your bad aim? He doesn't usually try to talk to me in class, so I knew it was important. I felt a piece of paper tickling the back of my neck and casually reached over my shoulder to grab it.

Scrawled on a ripped-out sheet of notebook paper in Sam's loose, wide writing were eight words:

> Saw a ghost last night. Meet after school?

Was he kidding? You can't just send a note like that and not expect a zillion questions. Here's what went back and forth between us. (I pasted it here with some new purple glue that's perfect for the job.)

> Saw a ghost last night. Meet after school?
>
> A real ghost?! Will ask Mom—Fergus might be making dinner >:(
>
> Real ghost! Looked like your dad. My mom can make dinner.

I know Sam didn't mean to upset me, but a ghost that looks like my dad is a pretty upsetting thing.

So I stared at the paper for a moment, letting my eyes go out of focus. Doing that helps me concentrate. Ideally,

I'd close my eyes completely, but that would attract Ms. Luna's attention. Relaxing my eyes was good enough. Once they lost focus, I could think clearly.

First, did I really think that Sam had seen a ghost?

Yes and no. I think Sam saw *something* he thought was a ghost. But our minds can play tricks on us. And it couldn't have been a real ghost. Because I'm old enough to know that ghosts aren't real—and that's a FACT.

Second of all, even if ghosts were real, the ghost couldn't be my dad. Because my dad is missing. And a ghost would mean something much worse. So it was obvious that Sam did not see a ghost. And the ghost he did not see was definitely not my dad.

But then I realized maybe he saw my dad in some kind of disguise that made him look like a ghost. I tapped my pen against my lips, mulling that over, when Ms. Luna broke into my thoughts.

"Hannah? Sam? Do either of you know the difference between an independent and dependent clause?" Ms. Luna was looking at us disapprovingly, her hands on her hips. My usual note-taking trance had been completely interrupted by Sam's message. I had no notes to glance down at, no previous memory to call on.

"Well, if you can't answer my question, is there something else that you'd like to share with the class?" Ms. Luna peered at my desk. Did she see me sliding the note between the pages of my book? Not sure.

"No, Ms. Luna," we said. I'd like to say that Sam and I are such close friends that we responded in perfect unison, but that's more like something that would happen in some sappy romance novel, not in real life. In reality, Sam spoke just slightly before me, making us sound all mashed up, like "NoMsNosLuMsNasLuna."

Mary's hand shot up like an arrow, and her beads clacked as she bounced in her seat.

"Yes, Mary?"

"Ms. Luna, an independent clause is a sentence. A dependent clause is a fragment." She turned toward me, victory scrawled across her face. One point for Mary.

"Correct. Now, one last thing—" Ms. Luna was interrupted by the piercing bell. "I guess we will save that for next class. See you tomorrow, everyone!"

During the ruckus of papers sliding into backpacks and chairs being pushed back, nobody noticed that I was more or less glued to my seat. Passing notes in class was "not like me." It was a *BAD KID* thing to do. It signaled disrespect—or at least that's how Ms. Luna would see it, and I actually *like* Ms. Luna because she always wears such cool dresses and has a little gecko tattoo on her ankle that makes her seem mature and worldly, like some explorer turned English teacher. And most of all, I thought Ms. Luna liked me, but would she still after catching me in the act? Once I start worrying about things, sometimes my thoughts swirl and build and it's hard for me to move on while they pile up.

My heart was spiraling—no, it was racing—and right when I thought I would never move again, Sam spoke up.

"Hey, sorry we got caught. I know that you hate getting in trouble. Nerd." He smiled, lightly punching my shoulder.

"No problem, but you could have told me during recess. Slacker."

"And miss out on the world's most intense round of soccer? No way! So, do you think you can get out of having dinner with Chef Spaghettini's evil twin?"

"I'll ask my mom." I swung my backpack over my shoulders, securing both straps. We were the last kids to leave, and I could see Ms. Luna smiling at us. She didn't hate me! The spiraling sensation went away.

I wanted to ask Sam more about the ghost to figure out what he really saw, but he was already rushing off.

Ms. Luna waved at me as I walked out of the classroom—but I was too deep in thought to wave back. My head wasn't up in the clouds; it was down in the graveyard, thinking about ghosts and why Sam would think that something (that didn't even exist) would look like my missing dad.

Journal, I'll update you later. I'm home now and Mom just walked in, and I need to ask her if I can go to Sam's. I'll be back later with some answers. Maybe I'll even be able to tell you a real-life ghost story. But don't count on it.

4
CONVERSATION WITH A POSSIBLE GHOST

As an investigator, it's crucial to remain objective, impersonal, and, most important, accurate. That's why it's a really good idea for investigators to make audio recordings of their meetings—that way, nothing is forgotten, which is helpful when you're hunting for clues. By the way, it's also a good thing for business people to do. My dad does it all the time with important meetings. He has this old-fashioned mini-tape recorder that he sets up in his office, and when he gets home from work, he listens to his meetings and types them all up. The typing part he calls *transcribing*.

I took his tape recorder and some tapes the week he went missing. I just wanted to hear his voice again. Sadly, only a few tapes had any notes. Most of them were blank. As upsetting as that was, the blank tapes came in handy for my meeting with Sam. We had decided to meet in

Sam's treehouse, where we would have privacy. After I got home, I transcribed the tape we used. I wanted to focus on the important stuff, so—just as a heads up—all the slanted stuff are the things we whispered to each other that weren't important. I included them for accuracy.

September 9: First Attempt to Contact a Ghost in Sam's Treehouse

Hannah: *Sam, is it recording?*

Sam: *I think so? It's spinning a lot. Is that how it's supposed to work?*

H: *Yes, Sam. Let's get going.*

S: *Wouldn't it be easier to video this with our phones?*

H: *Ghosts can mess up more modern electronics. Plus, it's super dark in here. You wouldn't see a thing. Have you considered making a window?*

S: *You know if I made a window, then my sisters would spy on us.*

H: *Okay. We will have to cut off a lot of this recording. I'll get started now.* Ladies and gentlemen, I am Hannah Edwards.

S: And I am Sam, local soccer legend and hero.

H: *Show-off.* And we are here today to seek answers and possibly record a supernatural phenomenon with Sam's

Ouija board. Now, yesterday evening, Sam here had an experience almost too supernatural—too horrifying—to be true. Take it away, Sam.

S: So, last night, I was biking home from soccer practice. I guess I forgot to zip up my bag, because when I took a sharp turn around the grain mill, my soccer ball fell out and rolled underneath the fence and into the mill. The door to the mill is usually closed, but some kids must have left it open. Some people might have cut their losses and run. The mill is kind of scary at night, but I'd lost like two other soccer balls this summer, and I really didn't feel like getting a new one. So I decided to chase after it. Anyways, long story short, when I got inside the mill, I saw a ghost.

H: Can you tell us more about the ghost?

S: Yeah, sure! So I went into the mill, and I realized I could see my breath, which was pretty weird. And then I felt like somebody was watching me. But I was on a mission, so I just started to look for my soccer ball—which shouldn't have rolled too far. Suddenly, I saw the ball rolling back toward me. Like somebody had kicked it. I looked in the direction that the ball came from, and I saw this tall, see-through figure who was all glowing around the edges. His face was a little blurry, but he looked like your dad, only he wasn't wearing his cowboy hat.

H: Were you scared?

> (Journal, when I asked Sam this question, his face muscles tightened before he answered me, and I could tell he was definitely scared.)

S: No. I wasn't scared. The ghost waved at me and smiled, and his mouth moved like he was talking to me, but I couldn't hear a word he said. I wanted to leave. But it was like he was holding me there and I couldn't move. I decided to ask him if he was Hannah's dad when I heard this LOUD honk outside, and the whole mill lit up from a truck's headlights. Just like that, the ghost disappeared—that's how I know it wasn't a real person. Anyways, long story short again, I'd left my bike in the middle of the road when I chased after my ball, and that was Joe (from Joe's Antique Emporium) in his truck, trying to get home, and he was not happy about my bike blocking the road.

H: Thanks, Sam. So, from what you've said, we can conclude that you had some sort of vision. Although you said the ghost looked like my dad, that's not possible because my dad is just missing. Another possibility is that you saw the Old Mill Ghost—who my dad's family may actually be related to.

> (Journal, I just want to make it clear here—I do not believe in ghosts. But Sam said he saw something, and number one, I would

never make fun of Sam. And number two, Dad says it's important to keep an open mind.)

H: Now, everyone who has ever stepped foot in Riverway is familiar with the Old Grain Mill and its ghost.

S: More like anybody who has ever talked to Rick—

H: For the record, the grain mill is rumored to be haunted by the ghost of an angry grain merchant. One hundred years ago, two brothers were fighting over their fair share of grain from the family farm. During the fight, the older brother fell into the grain vat, drowning in his own crop. Legend has it that his ghost still lurks in the mill, searching for his younger brother. However, nobody has seen any proof of this ghost. That's why Sam and I have a two-step plan. Step one: We are going to try to communicate with the spirit to figure out if he's real. Step two: If he is real, we are going to try to find out who he is.

S: Yeah, we're gonna use the Ouija board from Jemma's Gems that I got on the way home from school. Remember Jemma's Gems is where to go for the coolest toys. Joe's Antique Emporium is for buttheads.

H: *I thought you liked Joe's more.*

S: *Serves him right for almost hitting my bike! Plus, Jemma said she'd give me two dollars off if I gave her a shout-out.*

H: *All right.* The box says this board is filled with powerful magic—magic that, when used correctly, will thin the boundary between the physical and spiritual worlds, allowing spirits to move this "Mystical Triangle" and spell out words. Therefore, this tool is to be used by professionals only.

S: *Hannah, we aren't professionals.*

H: *Yes, we are!* Or at least they have to think we are, or else no one will believe us if we really do make contact with a ghost and actually let people listen to this tape. Now, Sam will tell everyone what we are doing to prepare for the communication.

S: I am now lighting the three emergency candles that I got from my last Scouts trip. We have put them in three corners of the treehouse. Don't worry about fires, though, because I also got a water bottle in case anything goes wrong.

S: Now, we both are sitting across from the board, and we both have our hands on the triangle piece that moves to select different letters. We are not holding hands. Do you hear that, everyone? NOT holding hands.

H: Good clarification, Sam. We are not, in any way, holding hands. Now, it is time to talk to the ghost. Should you go first since you saw the ghost?

S: Hello, Ghost, are you here?

> (In the interest of accuracy, Journal, Sam's voice shook a little when he said that.)

H: *That's not what you're supposed to say. You've got to be more dignified. Like: "Are there any spirits in the room with us tonight?"*

S: *That's not what the box says.*

H: *Well, I've watched more scary movies than you, and that's what they always say.*

S: *All right, I'll try again. Are there any spirits in the room with us tonight?*

> (Journal, Sam sounds much bolder now.)

H: Wait! Wait! Did you hear that? Listeners, there was just a big WHOOSH from outside. It could be the wind. But I'm not sure if there's wind out there tonight. Try that again, Sam.

S: ARE THERE ANY SPIRITS IN THE ROOM WITH US TONIGHT?

H: Whoa, yelling worked! Did you feel that?

S: I totally did.

H: Listeners, the triangle just moved. It is now covering the word "Yes."

S: We should ask another question, fast! I'm getting cold.

H: Me too! Listeners, the temperature has dropped considerably.

S: That's a sign that a ghost is here!

H: Unless the temperature is really dropping outside. So we're not sure if we can call it a supernatural occurrence yet. We are now moving the triangle back to the center of the board.

S: Spirit, can you speak to me?

H: Nothing is happening.

S: I'll yell it this time. SPIRIT, CAN YOU SPEAK TO ME?

H: Nothing. Maybe it just thinks that's a silly question because it already spoke to us by moving the triangle.

S: Okay . . . Oh, I know what to ask! Spirit, how were you killed?

H: Why would you ask that? How do you know it was killed? And, anyway, you should be finding out its name first.

S: Too late! Something is happening here.

[Some minor static and shuffling sounds.]

H: Are you doing that?

S: No, I swear—I am not!

H: *Listeners, the triangle is moving again, but very slowly, almost as though a third hand is dragging it toward a letter.*

Sam's mom: Sam! Hannah! What are you doing up there?

H: *Quick, blow out the candles! We don't want to get into trouble.*

S: *No, we have to finish. I'll just tell her to wait.* Moooooom! Please go away. We are trying to summon a ghost!

Sam's mom: WHAT? Sam and Hannah, come down here this instant. I've got dinner on the table. Chicken adobo.

> (Sam's family is Filipino, and his mom is an amazing cook. Sam suddenly looked like he wouldn't mind ending the séance.)

Sam's mom: Are those candles? In a treehouse? Are you trying to get yourselves killed?

S: One minute!

Sam's mom: No more minutes! Hannah has to go home. Her mother just called. It's getting late. You'd better get down here by the time I count to three. Otherwise, I'm coming up there—and you don't want that. One . . .

S: I guess we've got to go! I'll get the candles.

H: I'll hide the board! We don't want her to take it away.

Sam's mom: Two . . .

S: We're coming!

Sam's mom: Three! All right, that's it. I'm coming up.

H and S: No! We're coming down now!

End of recording

5
THE HAUNTED MATH CLASS

Between the ages of four and six, every kid—and I mean *every kid*—believes ghosts are real. When I was six, I was convinced my school was haunted. There were plenty of good reasons to think so. The building was big and spooky, with tiny little windows. And it was always empty at night, and that's Ghost City galore! Plus, Bruce, my babysitter's fourteen-year-old son, told me that the fence around the school wasn't there to keep kids in but to keep ghosts from getting out. "That's why the fence has those spiky posts! If the ghosts try to climb over, their clothing gets caught and they can't leave," he assured me. Which made perfect sense to a six-year-old.

The night he told me that, I had nightmares filled with the ghosts of janitors and teachers, all pressing their faces against the fence, trying to get out. Even worse, I realized that if I went to school the next day, the ghosts would be inside the yard with me!

In the morning, I begged my mom to *please* let me be homeschooled. But she just rolled her eyes, put another ham and cheese sandwich in my lunch bag, and, instead of asking what the problem was, said, "Hannah, I know school might be boring at times, but you'd be more bored here than at school with your friends."

I should have told her about the ghosts, but it felt too much like the little-kid things three-year-olds say, so I sucked it up and went. My dad was a bit more understanding. At least he asked me why I wanted to stay home.

"I just don't want to go," I said as he walked me there. "They keep us trapped in the yard with those spiky poles! And did you know—" I almost slipped, but I stopped myself.

"Did I know what?" he prompted, his eyes twinkling in a way that said, "I know what the *real* problem is." Mom always said that twinkle is what made him so good with his employees.

"Did you know that, um, the spiky poles were made to break kids' soccer balls on purpose and ruin their fun?" I had fooled him! I was sure of it!

"Oh, I'd always heard that the spiky poles prevented the ghosts from leaving," he said.

My feet suddenly stopped moving. He *did* know. Wait. Had he heard Bruce tell me that? Would Bruce get in trouble now? I waited to see if he would say something more, but he just took my hand and gently tugged on it, prompting me to keep moving.

"I remember the first time I heard about the schoolyard ghosts," he said. "I left the house and pretended I was going to school, but I actually went to the river to play. I decided I was never going back to school. I skipped class for a week—until the day I met the fisherman and told him about the ghosts. He explained that ghosts are usually lonely people who are lost and scared and want to go home. The fisherman said they approach people who are kind and friendly. 'Ghosts don't mean to scare you. If you ever see one, know that they are talking to you because they trust you to be nice enough to help them go home.'

"Once he told me that, I ran off to school, determined to help any ghosts I met," my dad continued. "I never did see any, though. Maybe, if you're lucky, you'll be able to do what I couldn't. Maybe you will find a ghost and help them get home! Does that sound like a plan?"

I nodded. Dad's story made me feel a lot better. Now I was really worried about these ghosts who were lost and away from home and stuck at *school*, of all places. I left my extra ham and cheese sandwich on the fence just in case they were hungry.

Up until Sam's recent story and the Ouija board incident, I had pretty much forgotten about ghosts. I'd outgrown them. I didn't believe in them or just didn't think about them. If something moved late at night or there were weird noises, or groans, or moans, my first thought wouldn't be, "Oh no! A ghost!" Most likely I'd say what my mom always says: "That's just the house settling." (Not that I know why a house would settle, but it seems like a wise adult phrase, so I use it, too.)

So . . . even after Sam and I sort of contacted the ghost two nights ago, I hadn't come around to the idea that ghosts were real. Did I really think the triangle had moved on its own? No, not really. It was probably the wind. That's why I overlooked some critical safety instructions and never ended the ritual officially. This, according to the Ouija board box, involves blowing out the candles, spreading salt around, and thanking the spirits for their help. If you don't follow these instructions, then the ghosts may be left wandering our earth, and—even worse—they can become attached to you. That last part wasn't on the box. It just happens *all the time* in scary movies.

Did I believe the safety instructions on the box? No, I didn't. But during math class today, it felt like a ghost had become attached to me. I know it's because Sam and I texted all night about our near-ghost encounter and now I'm imagining that everything is a ghost—the curtains in the living room, the steam rising from the pasta pot, the light shining from the lamppost across the street. The events from math class today, though, are slightly less easy to explain.

I kept trying to look at the whiteboard, but my eyes were drawn to the window in the far-left corner of the room. Outside, in the early morning light, a gnarled, thin branch that looked like a finger kept tapping on the glass. The longer I stared at it, the more convinced I was that, even if it was a tree branch now, this thing used to be a finger. Some poor creature was trapped inside the rough bark of that tree and was trying to say, "Hello! Come see me! Come free me! Why are you inside?" It needed me to talk to it and let it out. So sitting there was not just boring; it was the morally wrong thing to do!

And besides that, I could feel every muscle in my legs slowly melting away into a puddle. I was sure if I didn't stand up soon, the puddle of muscles would blend together and form a thick paste that would meld me to the plastic school chair forever. Right when I was about to ask if I could go to the bathroom (the perfect excuse for a quick schoolyard break), a voice rasped in my ear: "Hannah! Pay attention! She's about to call on you and ask you which symbol means 'greater than.' Remember the alligator."

That voice shocked my leg muscles back into solidity. I don't know how—I don't know why—but the voice sounded just like my dad's.

Before I could turn around to see if he was hovering at my ear, Ms. Knugen tapped her foot three times, which she only does when she is exasperated, sighed twice, and (while yawning) asked, "Hannah, since nobody else has raised their hand, can you come draw the right symbol on the board?"

"Absolutely," I said, my eyes darting around, looking for the source of the voice. I confidently walked over to the whiteboard and wrote:

$$7\frac{2}{3} > 7.55$$

It was an easy question when you know what's coming. I could clearly remember sitting at the kitchen table and laughing as my dad drew alligators all over my math homework. "See? The alligator's mouth is always hungry for the biggest meal. So it always faces the biggest number."

Ms. Knugen stared at the board, this time tapping her foot once (a sharp exclamation) and holding her chin. She reached out and slightly corrected one of the lines that I had drawn, which was, admittedly, a bit squiggly. Even though she said, "Correct," her voice lacked the tone of Ms. Luna's praise. Maybe I was just being paranoid—I was, after all, a little shaken by the mysterious voice.

The main question is, How did the voice know to tell me about the alligator? And why did it sound like my dad?

Journal, I know the answer. I just imagined it was my dad standing there because Sam had gotten me all worked up by saying the ghost looked like my dad. And because my dad was the last person to tell me about the alligator. And because I miss him.

Here's something else I know. My dad cannot be a ghost because he is alive. So I have to find out where he is and why he is having trouble getting back to us.

But here's something I don't know—where do I start? How do you find someone who has completely disappeared?

6
THE TERRIBLE STEW

"And that's why you should never look at any screen for more than twenty minutes. It'll make you go blind by the time you're my age. Several studies have shown it." Uncle Fergus dropped his fork with pride, convinced he had saved the next generation of youth (me) from certain blindness. As the fork clattered onto his empty plate, my mom shot him a look I was very familiar with. It said: "Interesting, but don't go overboard with the lecturing."

"Thank you for the advice." I tried to make my voice as genuine as possible. Fergus wasn't entirely wrong. I knew one of those studies he mentioned. (We learned about it last year in science class.) The actual fact was for every twenty minutes in front of the screen, you should look away from it for twenty seconds to prevent your eyes from getting too tired. But, hey, we all have a bit of a tendency to exaggerate.

Now Mom gave *me* a look. This one said: "Hannah, have you forgotten something?"

"And thank you for the lovely meal," I added, staring down at what might have passed for a stew (if stews only involved rice and beef). To give him some credit, this meal was clearly homemade, but I was starting to deeply regret my previous rudeness: At least Chef Spaghettini was edible.

"Thank you, Hannah. You've barely touched your food, though. You know, protein is very important for your developing brain." I tuned Fergus's next speech out. I figured it was Mom's turn to respond anyway. Since school started, I've felt—or I've hoped—that Mom was also beginning to see Fergus's constant visits as overstaying his welcome. A burst of laughter from my mother quashed my hopes. I poked at a piece of beef, noticing how it floated in the rice-broth mixture. Is meat supposed to float?

"Hannah, what about you? Did anything interesting happen in class today?" My mother redirected the conversation to me.

"No, nothing out of the ordinary." I doubted that this was the right time to tell her about the mysterious voice in math class. Besides, the more I thought about it, the more I was certain I'd imagined it. Dad once told me that the power of suggestion was the biggest superpower in the world. All the ghost talk and the séance must have affected me. Plus, if I told Mom about the voice, then I'd have to tell her about how I hadn't been paying attention, and I definitely didn't want to do that.

"Nothing? Well, that's no good," Fergus piped in. "You know, every day—every lesson—is a learning experience. I've often thought about that myself. In fact, if I could go back to school, I'd pay a whole lot more attention in class."

Even though I knew it was impossible, "pay a whole lot more attention in class" felt directed at me. But there was no way Fergus could know how distracted I can be in class, and how it's gotten worse since Dad disappeared.

"Very insightful." I tried not to sound too sarcastic—adults hate that. "I'm full. Can I go now?" I stood up before waiting for permission, eagerly carrying my "stew" to its rightful place—the compost bin.

"Are you sure you've had enough?" Mom asked, slowing the stew's path to the garbage.

"Yeah, I'm sure."

"It seems like you're in a bit of a rush. Do you have an important project you're working on?" If only she knew.

"No, nothing really. I was just going to call Sam and see if he wants to do something before it gets too dark."

"Okay," Mom said, but her voice had that *there is something else we need to talk about* tone. "Before you call Sam, have you finished all your homework?"

"There's not much right now." That wasn't entirely

a lie. I had some math worksheets and a book report to start, but those wouldn't take me much time at all. Plus, I had to wait until I felt motivated to do those. Once I got this whole Ghost Theory out of the way, I'd be able to focus more. I was sure of it.

"Oh, I was just a bit surprised because you usually dive right in before school gets really busy. I've just noticed that you haven't been doing much schoolwork, that's all." Mom seemed genuinely concerned, as if she didn't want to upset me. Meanwhile, Fergus was leaning back on his chair with a smug look, clearly perceiving all this as a "learning moment," thanks to him.

"Don't worry, Mom. The stuff this year is a *total* repeat from last year." (Which, so far, was true.) "I'll finish my work on time—I always do."

"All right, so long as everything is under control."

I nodded enthusiastically, finally depositing the stew in the trash. As I turned to head up to my room, however, I was interrupted by the most beautiful words a hungry kid can hear. "Don't you want to stay for dessert? I made brownies." Mom brought a plate of them to the table.

Journal, let me tell you, brownies would make me tolerate *any* annoying houseguest. I whipped around and returned to my seat. I took one off the plate and was about to savor the first bite when the doorbell rang, and I almost dropped the brownie on the floor.

"Who could that be?" Fergus asked, his voice oddly low and territorial, like how *dare* somebody else try to come over here? My mom, for her part, didn't seem confused at all.

"It's Rick. He likes to come by on Wednesdays to update me." Mom headed to the front door and stepped outside, leaving me and Fergus sitting at the table in awkward silence.

Mom likes to meet Rick on the porch. She used to invite him in for tea, but there's not much point in that anymore—his updates are finished before the water even boils. Also, she can see that Rick's updates upset me. Little does she know, I'm on the case now, too.

Mom returned seconds later, like clockwork.

"Any news?" Fergus asked, his voice unusually gentle. Mom shook her head.

"That's not a surprise. Did they at least post more **MISSING PERSON** signs?" I asked.

"Hannah, Rick and his team are trying their best," Mom answered.

"You know, police work is very hard. Seventy-five percent of cases go unsolved," Fergus said, but, with a quick glance at my mom, he added, "not that that will happen with this case."

"If they gave the case to somebody who cared, like me, I bet they'd have more leads. It's like they've forgotten that their job is to do more than visit us once a week. It's to find Dad." I stuffed the brownie in my face, looking defiantly at Fergus. "Maybe I'll help them. Maybe I'll start looking for clues."

I didn't mean to say that. I didn't want anyone to know what I was up to, but I was so angry it just slipped out.

Fergus opened his mouth to say something, but my mom touched his arm and gave him a stern look.

I gulped down the brownie and cleared away my plate. "Thanks for dessert, Mom, delicious as always. Can I go upstairs now?"

Mom nodded. As I crept up to my room, I heard her and Fergus whispering to each other, and I was sure they were talking about me. But I didn't care. I needed to focus on the bigger picture—the sooner Dad got home, the sooner we didn't have to eat Fergus's terrible dinners.

7
WORSE THAN GHOSTS

"Rick came over last night with the same old report: 'No new developments,'" I told Sam. "I don't think he's doing enough to find my dad. That's why I want to investigate my father's disappearance." We were sitting under a pine tree near the back of the schoolyard—a place where we'd hung out since first grade.

"Rick's a good guy. I'm sure he's trying," Sam replied. His voice was level and annoyingly grown-up, like my mom's. "Plus, he has all those police tools to help him out." That was more like him.

"Yes, but he has to deal with every case in town! He can't spend all his time looking for my dad. Plus, I have personal insight into the case. It'll help me look for clues."

"That makes sense." Sam nodded. "And we have a head start." His voice brightened. "We already have our first clue! Our ghost!"

"Actually, Sam, I have to tell you something about that. I don't really believe in ghosts."

"I know the ghost thing seems unbelievable, especially since you haven't seen one yet. But what about the other night? I think we contacted one. And what about the voice you heard in math class yesterday?" Sam picked up a pine cone and began studying its scales.

"I could have imagined that voice," I said.

Journal, that was the start of my ghost conversation with Sam today. But something else ghostly happened at my locker this morning, and I didn't want to tell Sam about it because it would support his Ghost Theory, and I needed him to keep an open mind. Anyway, it was sort of like the voice. It was hard to know if it was real or if I had imagined it.

"Fair enough," Sam replied. "Maybe the voice wasn't a ghost. But I'm telling you, Hannah. I did see something in the old mill. I didn't imagine that." He weighed the pine cone in his hand, winding up to pitch it like a baseball. "How far do you think I can throw this?"

"Probably not too far. It would just hit a branch and fly back into your face. And if it did go far, you'd reveal our hideout."

The tree we were sitting under gave us the right mix of privacy and comfort. Due to years of school budget cutbacks, the trees in the field back here are not maintained, so the lower branches form a thick mesh around the base of "our tree." But if you know just the right spot, you can dodge the worst of the sharp branches and creep right up to the trunk, where there is a surprising amount of space. Although it's getting a bit cramped now that we are bigger.

"Yeah, you're probably right." Sam started picking apart the pine cone. "So, what's our next step, Chief Investigator Hannah?"

"Well, we don't want to jump to any rash conclusions. I'm sure there's a logical explanation for the voice I heard. And for the triangle on the Ouija board." It's funny how, when you get a bit older, your adult brain tells you that you need to find the *facts* and determine a *logical explanation*.

"All right, so what do we know?" Sam asked.

Journal, here is what we came up with:

A LIST OF THINGS WE KNOW
1. Sam says he saw a ghost that looked like my father.
2. Sam thinks we contacted a ghost with the Ouija board. I think we made contact with the wind.
3. I heard a voice that sounded like my dad's, but it probably wasn't his actual voice.

"There's one more thing," I said. I decided I had to tell Sam about what happened at my locker this morning. One thing about lists is that it is crucial that they contain all the important information. An incomplete list is like a puzzle with a missing piece. Imagine holding the last piece in your hand and not putting it in place—that's basically impossible! So, despite my desire to stay level-headed and not add too much fuel to Sam's "ghost" fire, I had to tell him.

"The things in my locker are moving," I said. "Usually, my textbooks are organized in order of classes, but when I came to school this morning, they were arranged alphabetically. I'm not sure if my eyes were playing tricks on me, but in the right light, it almost seemed like they sparkled."

Far from being shocked, Sam nodded and began to list a series of facts, counting off each one on his fingers.

1. Sparkle is a clear sign of ectoplasm.
2. It's the mucus ghosts leave behind when they touch things.
3. These facts lead to one logical explanation: You, Hannah Edwards, are being haunted.

See, Journal. That's why I didn't want to tell Sam. I knew he would say that. But it can't be true. Ghosts aren't real. There must be another explanation.

A branch on the tree shook, covering us in pine needles. I turned toward the movement and noticed a pair of sneakers poking in from the lower branches. Somebody was listening to us. Sam gingerly reached toward the shoes (probably to untie the shoelaces and prevent an easy escape). Right when he did, the shoes moved a bit to the left.

"Sam, I can see your hand!" said the voice attached to the sneakers.

"Well, stop spying on us then! What do you want?" Sam called out.

The shoes moved again, and Tim's face appeared in their place. Except he was upside-down, bending over to peek inside. He had one finger pressed against the bridge of his black-framed eyeglasses so they wouldn't fall off. "I just heard what you said, and I want to tell you guys that you are wrong about Hannah's locker and the ghost."

"How do you know?" Sam asked.

"Well, since I am older than you two, I have a unique perspective on these kinds of situations."

I rolled my eyes. Tim was born in December, but his parents held him back a year, so he is technically older than us, and he never lets anyone forget it. Even though I really wanted to hear what Tim had to say about the ghost, I didn't want help from someone who was snooping. "I think we've got it covered, but thanks. Besides, we don't need help from a spy."

"Oh, is that so? Well then, you clearly don't need me."

Tim's face disappeared, and his feet turned to walk away. "You know, it is a pity. I'm the Hall Monitor now. I could be very helpful."

That was it. I caved. Having the hall monitor on your side is always a good idea.

"Tim! Wait!" I cried. "What do you know?"

"I will tell you, on one condition. Um . . . can I . . . um . . . hang out with you under this pine tree?" he asked.

"Done!" I said. "Why don't you come under the tree with us right now?"

Sam quickly directed Tim around the worst of the branches, and, within seconds, he was sitting next to us, tugging on his shirt so we wouldn't see the buttons pulling across his belly.

"Okay, so I heard you reviewing the locker facts and Sam's conclusion that you're being haunted. And, given those facts, yes, the only logical explanation is a ghost. But what would you say if I told you that you don't have all the facts?" Tim asked.

"Like what?" I said.

"As you both know, I am the Hall Monitor." (Journal, you can practically hear the capital letters when Tim says this. That's why I'm writing them here.) "It is an important position with a lot of responsibility, but I try my best not to let it get to my head. Nevertheless, because I am the Hall Monitor, I am allowed to patrol the halls for an extra two minutes after the bell rings to make sure everyone is in class. A good Hall Monitor ensures that, during these patrols, his feet don't clomp on the tiles." (Journal, Riverway High frowns upon clompers.) "And he is stealthy—seen only by truants moments before he issues them a warning for being late. As a result, most people forget that I'm even there. I am, in many ways, like a ghost." He looked at me knowingly. "Don't worry, I am not your ghost, but I know somebody who is haunting you."

"Tim, with all due respect, can you just spit it out!" I said. There is nothing worse than a storyteller who just drags on and on.

"I'm just trying to build suspense, but okay, here I go. You are being haunted by none other than Ms. Grant!"

Ms. Grant is one of our two school counselors. She says she is "always here to help us" if there are any problems, and she seems nice, but I am wary of anyone who tries too hard to make kids like them. She reminds me of the witch from "Hansel and Gretel," but her house is made from construction paper and smiley face stickers instead of candy. Rather than being "welcoming" and "cheerful," her bright clothing reminds me of toxic frogs, who are covered in bright colors that warn predators they are poisonous. Plus, she secretes things, like a frog, although her secretions are mainly made up of glitter, which she sheds as she walks down the halls to mark her territory.

Her long nails are claws, coated with protective polish and sharpened to a point. The worst part is her smell: a sickly sweet scent, like vanilla and rotten fruit that has been kept in a plastic bag in the back of the fridge.

And one more thing. She has a huge crush on my uncle Fergus. I noticed it last month during the town hall meeting, and now I can't unsee it. First, she strode into the meeting two minutes late, trying to dazzle everyone in an unusually bright outfit: a neon green and orange polka-dot T-shirt and a matching green pencil skirt. She completed the look with orange lipstick and purple eyeliner. Instead of quietly taking a seat, she stood near the entrance, holding a hand over her eyes as if she were searching for treasure. Upon seeing my uncle with us in the front row, she waved wildly, rushed over, and made my mom move her purse so she could squeeze in next to Fergus.

Whenever my uncle spoke in the meeting (which was too often, in my opinion), she cheered. (Let me make this clear, Journal. No one cheers at these meetings.) To make matters worse, when the meeting was over, she insisted that he walk her to her car because "who knows what's out there this time of night—the town isn't as safe as it once was." (I'm pretty sure that comment was about my dad.) And when they got to her car, she kissed him. It was on the cheek. But still. Gross!

"I know it's shocking," Tim said, "but it is true. Hannah, you mentioned changes in your locker. As a teacher, Ms. Grant has access to all our locker combos. Also, as you know, there is nothing she loves more than alphabetizing things to 'keep them neat and tidy.' Finally, you mentioned sparkles on your textbooks. What is Ms. Grant's writing implement of choice?"

"Glitter pens," I said.

"Pink glitter pens. And yesterday, I was on hall duty when I saw you walk away from your locker and head to history class. Moments later, I saw Ms. Grant tiptoeing toward your locker. When you turned the corner, she quickly opened it and started rummaging around inside. I'd never seen a teacher—or any school employee, for that matter—going through a student's locker. But as Hall Monitor, I am well aware that Ms. Grant outranks me, so I decided the best course of action was to simply stroll by and say hello. When she heard me, she jumped right out of her skin. She told me that I 'had frightened her,' that she was 'just grabbing a book for Hannah,' and that she thought she saw George trying to duck out of his math class. As I raced after the potential truant, a few things struck me as odd—why did she feel the need to explain herself to me? When would you have had time to tell her that you were missing a book? Since when was book-grabbing part of her duties? But now that I've heard your story, everything is falling into place. For some reason—I don't know why—Ms. Grant is looking into you." Tim gazed at me expectantly, as if I knew the answers to his questions.

"I guess that solves one mystery and creates a thousand more," I said. A massive understatement for me.

The first lunch bell rang. BLEEEEEEEEEENG. There would be two more rings before we were late.

"Well, that's my signal. I'd love to stay and chat, but I've got to finish my rounds of the playground. Look for any potential loiterers." Tim crouched (you can't stand up under the tree) and started to dust himself off. "Sorry, Sam . . . if you don't mind . . . can you . . ." Tim pointed toward what he thought was the exit.

"Guide you out? Right this way." Sam held up a branch. As Tim crawled away, Sam asked me, "What are we going to do, Hannah?"

"As I see it, we have two missions now. One, I need to determine why Ms. Grant is going through my locker. Two, we still need clues to search for my father."

Journal, I have to tell you, I was relieved to hear about Ms. Grant at my locker because it supported my No Ghost Theory. But when I looked at our Things We Know list again, most of them had to do with Sam's ghost. So before I could move on, I had to disprove his Ghost Theory once and for all. Otherwise, it would keep circling my brain, and I wouldn't be able to concentrate on finding real clues.

So—and I can't believe I suggested this—I told Sam we should meet after school today and have another séance.

"As for Ms. Grant," I said, "leave her to me." So Sam headed off to class, and I'm here, finishing up my notes on the case. I want to get them down while they're fresh.

Journal, you're now up to speed on the newest developments. The last bell just rang, so I've got to run. Tim is both a powerful new ally and a strict hall monitor—I won't get any free passes from him.

8
AN APPOINTMENT WITH MS. GRANT, THE GLITTER DRAGON

~~One thing that makes me happy:~~
~~One thing that makes me sad:~~
~~My new goal for today:~~

Once I'd finished my last entry, I raced to my locker to get my books. I must have messed up the combination at least four times. (Why does that always happen when you're in a rush?) Just as the lock opened with a satisfying click, a cloud of perfume ripped my journal out from under my arm.

"What is this?" Ms. Grant asked in a voice as sweet as her perfume. "A diary?"

"No, Ms. Grant. It's a journal," I said.

"How very exciting." She started flipping through the pages, then turned to the first page and read the inscription on the cover. "'Hannah's Grief Journal. Lots of Love, Mom.' Oh, Hannah, you should have mentioned that it is a grief journal. Those are *very* different things from normal journals. In fact, if you'd told me that it was a grief journal, I never would have taken it from you. Grief is a *very* private thing." She said *private* as though it was personally directed at me, like I'd never understood what *private* meant until she said it. "But, Hannah, you're not *using* it right."

"Wait, is there a way to use the journal correctly?" I was genuinely curious. I hadn't really given the idea of a proper grief journal much thought at all. As you know, I'd just thrown it on the floor and then decided to use it for my detective work. If there is a right way to do something, then I always want to know what that is.

"Yes. Of course. There is always a right way to use a journal. Journals are some of the most powerful cognitive tools known to humankind. Let me just find my pen." She started rummaging through her purse, a purple sequined atrocity that was probably designed to blind her enemies during battle. I made a mental note to look up *cognitive* in a dictionary when I got home.

"Oh, silly me. Here it is!" She pulled out a pen from behind her ear and held its cap in her mouth. Turning to the newest empty page, she wrote the three sentences (or "prompts," as she called them) that you saw at the beginning of this entry:

> ~~One thing that makes me happy:~~
> ~~One thing that makes me sad:~~
> ~~My new goal for today:~~

She returned my journal with a look of immense satisfaction. Clearly, these three lines meant the world to her.

"These seem . . ." I began, a bit annoyed that she just *wrote* in *my* journal.

"Important?" She smiled.

"Simple."

Her smile quickly turned into a frown, and her face began to crinkle.

"Simple? Well, they may seem simple, but answering these three questions is the key to a meaningful life. Trust me, they are more useful than filling this journal with doodles and scribbles."

As she spoke, little bits of spit flew from her mouth and landed on the pages. I've never heard of a water-breathing dragon, but if there is one, then Ms. Grant is *definitely* related to it. She paused and raised her eyebrows, waiting for some sort of response. But I was busy staring at her bag. One of the sequins had flipped the wrong way, making it slightly less sparkly than the rest. I really wanted to reach out and flip it right-way up, but something told me that would *not* be a good idea. After a few seconds of silence, she took a deep breath and plastered on her usual smile.

"Well, Hannah, I know that your classes start soon. I'd like to explain how to make the journal work a little bit better. Or we could just . . ." I know that she said something else, but I was too focused on the sequin to be able to make out what words she said. It was calling out to me. "Hannahhhhhhh," it said, "flip me back overrrrrrrrrrrr. I miss my other sequin frienddddddsssssss."

"Hannah? Does that sound good?" The sharp, inquisitive tone in her voice shocked me out of my trance.

"Oh, yes, that sounds good, Ms. Grant." If there's one thing I've learned, it's that you should *never* tell an adult you didn't hear what they said, because then they'll give you a lecture on paying attention. It's never happened to me, personally, because I'm too quick, but I've seen it happen to Sam before. It's better to just agree and move on.

"Fantastic! I will see you after school today. Three o'clock—can't wait!" Ms. Grant turned and clip-clopped away, a new cloud of perfume wafting in my direction as she left. The single non-flipped sequin bounced slightly, doomed to its life in isolation.

I had no idea what I'd agreed to. I was, of course, terrified, as anybody would be after an encounter with a creature as poisonous as Ms. Grant. Ms. Grant's appearance at my locker was no coincidence. She had clearly been planning yet another locker heist—but why?

As I sat through the next couple of classes, all I could think about was the meeting. Had Ms. Grant mentioned anything other than journaling? Did her snooping at my locker mean I had done something wrong? And, if I had done something wrong without knowing that it was wrong, was it really my fault? Well, of course it would be—I should instinctively *know* better if I am a *GOOD KID*.

In my last class, I was so busy running through a list of everything I'd done since school started—everything that could have been wrong—that I didn't even notice when the final school bell rang. Sam must have poked me with his pencil a dozen times before I finally jolted out of my thoughts.

"Stop that!" I snapped, quickly grabbing my things. I hoped that I wasn't late for the appointment with Ms. Grant already.

"Are you still down for our séance after school?" Sam asked.

Right. I'd forgotten about that.

"We're probably going to have to do it tomorrow," I said. "Tim was right about Ms. Grant—the glitter dragon herself cornered me at my locker after lunch. I've got to see her now."

"Oh man. Did she say what she wanted?"

"Not exactly. But I think I'm about to find out," I said. Then I turned and headed down the hall to the dragon lady's evil lair.

9
CAUGHT IN THE DRAGON'S CLUTCHES

I arrived at Ms. Grant's office barely on time and stopped at her office door. It looked like a construction-paper fairy had puked on it. There were hundreds of old comics cut out from the *Riverway Rooster* newspaper, at least eighteen smiley-face stickers, and four old "Hang in There" cat posters covered in Sharpie-marker vandalism—mostly eyeglasses and mustaches. We're not sure why she doesn't take them down.

She had traced over her nameplate with glitter glue, making it almost illegible. Most students identified her office by the pungent scent of a pumpkin spice diffuser and the sound of Beethoven seeping out from under the door. Just below the nameplate, there was a yellowing clear plastic letter holder filled with lime-green sheets. The box was labeled *Go Ahead—Take One! I Won't Tell Anyone* in gold glitter pen. Rumor had it that these lime-green sheets had a white **FOR PARENTS AND GUARDIANS** counterpart, but they were locked away in Ms. Grant's **ADULTS ONLY** filing cabinet.

As I knocked on her door, a shower of gold glitter fell to the ground. I knocked again, and the Beethoven paused. I was hit by a tsunami of fragrance as Ms. Grant opened the door. Have you ever inhaled the color orange? It was like that.

"Hannah! Come on in!" She smiled, a dragon welcoming its prey into its lair. "I've been looking forward to this all day." I gulped and stepped inside.

Ms. Grant's office was less of an office than a storage space for cushions. There were no chairs for visitors, no tables, no bookshelves—just dozens of cushions covering every available surface. She did have one steel filing cabinet, but its drawers were blocked by two particularly heavy looking cushions.

Ms. Grant sat cross-legged on a pink sequined cushion and gestured that I do the same. I chose a furry green one. (It was likely made from the pelt of some rare animal that had accidentally wandered into the dragon's clutches.) My knees immediately went to my chest. As I struggled to not drown in fur, Ms. Grant calmly continued.

"How has your day been, Hannah? Anything exciting happen in class?" Her voice was almost as sweet as the pumpkin spice.

"It's been good, Ms. Grant," I piped up, surfacing from the sea of fur. If this green creature had been a gentle animal in life, it was not in death. It clearly intended on eating me whole. I slightly adjusted my hips, and the green cushion fought back violently, throwing me forward onto my left elbow.

Ms. Grant, unaffected by my battle, continued to speak in a slow, even tone. "Just good? Is there anything that you want to tell me? You know you can tell me anything."

I could not have responded without getting a mouthful of fur, so I hoped she recognized that the bobbing of the cushion was caused by my nodding.

"You might find my sheet helpful to get us started."

I heard a series of shuffling and scrapes. Through the forest of green fur, I could just make out Ms. Grant, unzipping a rainbow cushion, grabbing the key to the filing cabinet, and standing to unlock the top drawer. She opened it only a crack—not enough that she had to move the two big cushions—and plucked one of those lime-green sheets of paper with her talons (I mean with her nails) from the drawer. As she turned around, she slammed the drawer shut and hid the key in her palm.

"Here you go!" She leaned over and offered me the paper with a smile. "These are on my door, but I don't think I've ever seen you take one. Read it!"

I extended an arm out from the fur forest and managed to grab hold of the sheet, which made me lose my balance and almost tumble onto Ms. Grant's feet. She didn't comment on my fall but winced when she heard the paper crumple slightly in my fist. For one tense second, I thought she was going to get mad at me for my carelessness. Instead, she exhaled slowly and leaned back on her pink sequined throne.

"Well? Are you going to read it? Ms. Luna says you are *quite* the good speed reader. I can even time you if that would make it more fun!"

The idea of creating a competition energized her. An evil glint in her eyes suggested that she would be very happy if I lost. Not because she would win, but because losing would make me sad, and then we could talk about why I was sad instead of the important things, like why she was rummaging around my locker. Ms. Grant was clearly not the person to challenge to battle. How many spelling-bee knights and speed-reading wizards had she consumed in this office? Who knows?

"That's okay, Ms. Grant," I said as a I rolled off the green cushion and onto a slippery blue one. The green cushion immediately popped back into shape, clearly proud that it had bested its rider. "I'm very tired today, so I'd rather read at a slower pace." I tried to stabilize myself on the blue cushion, which, although less overtly hostile than the green one, proved to be very slippery.

"Oh? Tired?" Ms. Grant inquired, raising a single eyebrow. You could almost see smoke starting to seep out of her nostrils. She sensed weakness, but I refused to take the bait and instead just read the sheet (which barely took any time). I've taped it here.

FOR KIDS:

Hello, Future Friends—yes, friends, because that's how I see you! My name is Ms. Grant, but you can call me Ginger.

As a guidance counselor, my job isn't to tattle to your parents or guardians; it's to talk to you with *complete confidentiality*. Confidentiality is a fancy way of saying that I am really good at keeping secrets. Think of me as a big, friendly safe.

I know it can be hard to talk to a grown-up about your problems, but—trust me—I am here to help! Come by my office anytime, and we can talk about homework, the best pizza in town, and your crushes. Remember: My lips are sealed!

See you soon!

Ginger

Ms. Grant sat completely still while I read the paper. I could feel her eyes boring into my skull and made a mental note to ask Sam if dragons have X-ray vision. When I looked up, she pounced.

"So, as you can see, I'm really here to talk about anything and everything! Do you have any questions?" Before I could answer, she added, "Oh, and call me Ginger!"

I racked my brain for the right thing to say. I wanted to be polite—to find a way to ask about her locker break-in without seeming rude—but I also felt that the longer I sat in that room, the more orange my lungs would become. The orange would seep into my blood and sink into my joints, paralyzing me from the inside out. Thinking about the orange made my legs shake. I wanted to run, to get some fresh air and escape this strange orange land with the furry green creature and the slippery blue cushion and the forbidden filing cabinet and this dangerous dragon. I took a deep breath and decided on a straightforward approach. "Why am I here, Ms. Grant?" I asked.

Ms. Grant's eyes widened slightly. Smoke practically blew out of her flared nostrils. I began to feel sympathy for the green-cushion creature—Ms. Grant's angry face was probably the last thing it had seen before it died. For a second, she looked like she was going to erupt and engulf me in flames. Then, just like lots of grown-ups I knew, she suddenly hid her feelings and put on a mask of mild pleasure. "I appreciate the directness, Ms. Edwards." She spat out my last name like it was coated in acid. (Note: Ask Sam if dragons spit out acid.)

"Now, all the teachers here at Riverway High have been *very* sympathetic to your recent loss. We all know that it is *very* hard to lose somebody at such a young age. As you know, it is my job to make sure that *every* student feels safe—at school and, in some cases, at home. Your father's disappearance is a *very* big change in your life. Journaling, when done correctly, can be a useful tool for processing things, but just like any tool in a toolbox, we need to know how to use it. My goal for these sessions is to provide you with a how-to guide."

As she said the ominous plural *sessions*, I slipped off the blue cushion and onto my butt. She glared at me, as if to say, "Can't you stay still for *one* second? My time is *very* valuable and what I am saying is *very* important."

"I've created a series of guiding questions," she went on, "but I always like to begin these conversations by giving you the opportunity to free-associate. Say anything that comes to mind about how the idea of this toolbox makes you *feel*."

"Why were you looking in my locker?" I'd been sitting on the question so long that it slipped out from under me—not unlike the blue cushion.

"Looking in your locker? Hannah, that is a very *serious*

allegation. What gave you that *silly* idea?" Ms. Grant's voice reached a deadly supersonic pitch. Dragons were a lot more dangerous than I'd initially thought.

"I have my sources." I knew that my answer was too vague and maybe too snippy, but I didn't want to tattle on Tim. "And there was glitter on my textbooks. My newly alphabetized textbooks." That was a bit better.

Ms. Grant tilted her head to the side, then looked up to the left and bit her lip just slightly—just enough for me to see her pronounced canines, a reminder that her bite matched her bark.

"Well, Hannah, I will admit that I have been occasionally visiting your locker, hoping to catch you in between classes. Given the recentness of your loss and the sensitivity of your case, I didn't want to make a public announcement over the intercom or call you out of class. If you'd prefer that I do so in the future, that can *certainly* be arranged."

The idea of Ms. Grant's syrupy voice calling out my name over the school-wide intercom made me shiver.

"Now that I think about it, there may have hypothetically been a time when your locker was left open—wide open. And I will admit that I was entranced—we counselors like to joke that lockers are the windows into students' souls. And I might have tidied up some things if it was messy enough to be a hazard. And, of course, I would have locked your locker afterward, not to cover my tracks but to protect your belongings."

At this point, she was gesturing wildly, like Sally Sue when she played Juliet for the Fall Harvest Festival. I believe that the *Riverway Rooster* described this performance as "overblown and self-aggrandizing"—whatever that meant.

The orange must have been getting to my head because Ms. Grant's answer seemed plausible. I'm always leaving cupboards open at home (much to Mom's annoyance). I very well could have gotten caught up in something and wandered away from my locker before locking it. Maybe Tim didn't see that my locker door was open. And it wasn't really that bad—it's not like my textbooks were harmed by the forced alphabetization. Plus, from Ms. Grant's dramatic performance, her locker-escapades seemed unlikely to reoccur. Now, I just had to get out of there before I drowned in cushions—or turned into one myself.

"Hannah?" Ms. Grant waved a taloned hand before my eyes. "Where did you go just now?" She made unwavering eye contact, not to show that she wanted to connect with me—no—but to show that she desperately wanted to devour any juicy information she might wring from my brain.

"Oh. I'm not really sure, I guess." I doubted that Ms. Grant would appreciate my opinion on her acting. And

I didn't want to tell her about my mind wandering. She needed to think that, other than my loss, everything in my head was perfectly all right.

She clicked her tongue. "You know, Hannah, sometimes when we are hurt, we put up walls around ourselves. Walls that prevent us from being in the present. Walls that prevent us from connecting. Don't worry. I am here to break down those walls."

The idea of Ms. Grant breaking down my walls was more threatening than comforting—more like a dragon blasting into a castle than a knight in shining armor asking me to let down my hair.

"And I have just the exercise to do it." Ms. Grant leaped up from her sequined throne, reached for a remote, and pressed play. A chorus of birdsong blasted from a speaker.

"Isn't that calming? Now, Hannah, our first exercise is a vision exercise. I want you to imagine yourself as a pillow."

My cushion nightmare was coming true. The transformation was beginning.

"Imagine yourself becoming restful. Just like a pillow. Soft and saggy."

"*Soffffttt and saggggyyyyyyyyy,*" the cushions seemed to chime out in chorus. "*Become one of us.*"

"Say it with me, Hannah. 'I am soft and saggy. I am relaxed.'"

Sam, if you are reading this, then I most definitely did *not* say, "I am soft and saggy." I didn't do it for five minutes. And then, if I did, it was just so we could hurry up and end the session.

"Now, doesn't that feel refreshing? Don't you feel better?" The birdsong ended, turning into a chorus of ocean waves.

"I feel different." I checked my arms to see if they were sprouting green fur. Although I think I'd be a purple cushion; that's more my style.

"Different is good! Now, feel free to use this tool *whenever* you need it. I think that's enough for today! I'll be seeing you again, I hope!"

Ms. Grant herded me out, not noticing my stumbling on the green cushion (who likely resented me for escaping before the transformation was complete). "Remember—my door is always open."

As I stepped into the hallway, I saw the chess club standing across the way. They were staring at us (possibly paralyzed by their fear of Ms. Grant). Mary, their ringleader, smiled and waved at me.

With that wave, I bolted from Ms. Grant's office without saying thank you. Even though I didn't see her face and I couldn't have heard her above the sound of my feet pounding the tile floor, I could have sworn smoke escaped from her nostrils as she watched me run away.

"How ungrateful!" she probably muttered.

Not that I cared. I'd wasted time by meeting with Ms. Grant, who, by the way, never told me how to journal properly, leading me to conclude that this was bait to lure me into her evil cushion-transforming grasp for who knows what reason.

Being seen leaving her office made things even worse. The chess club's stares had shown no malice, but, in some ways, curiosity is worse than malice.

What did she do wrong? they had to be thinking. Rumors would start, and before you knew it, my good reputation would meet a quick end. Believe me, I've seen it happen. So now I needed to try harder to be normal.

Journal, safe to say I will *not* be talking to Ms. Grant ever again.

10
ANOTHER CONVERSATION
WITH A GHOST
(AND THE DEATH OF THE TRIANGLE)

September 12: Second Attempt to Contact a Ghost in Sam's Treehouse

Sam: *So, why did Ms. Grant want to meet you?*

Hannah: *Just stuff about my dad. My recent loss. I don't want to talk about it right now.*

> (Journal, even though I tell Sam everything, the meeting with Ms. Grant was pretty embarrassing, and there are some things that I want to keep to myself.)

S: *All right, we are rolling.*

H: *Okay, let's try to do it quickly this time, before your mom finds out. We are here today to try to contact the ghost again. Sam is here to prove it's real. I am here to prove it's not. Sam's mom confiscated all our candles after our* last séance, so we are making do with glow sticks. Sam, I guess you should start the glow sticks?

S: On it!

[Cracking noises.]

S: *You know, the green glow is way creepier than the candles. The ghost will probably like that.*

H: The board is ready. We are in position. Sam, why don't you ask again?

S: Are there any spirits in the room with us tonight?

[Silence.]

S: I think we should say something different. Maybe they're tired of answering the same questions. Why don't we invite them in first?

H: Spirit that Sam saw in the old mill, we invite you to join us in Sam's treehouse. Do you accept our invitation?

[Static noises.]

S: Look! Do you see that? The triangle is moving.

H: "Yes."

> (Just so you know, Journal. It really did look like the triangle was moving. Only our fingertips were touching it. I have to admit, my heart started to race, but I tried to play it cool.)

H: It looks like the spirit has accepted our invitation. Spirit, are you the one they call the Old Mill Ghost?

S: It's getting cold in here.

H: Yeah, I'm freezing.

S: And my nose is running.

H: The board is shaking.

S: *Sorry, that's probably me. I should have worn a jacket.*

H: *We'll know for next time!* SPIRIT, ARE YOU THE ONE THEY CALL THE OLD MILL GHOST?

S: It's moving! The ghost says, "No."

H: Did you do that, Sam? Did you maybe push that to "No" even though you didn't mean to?

S: I didn't, Hannah. I swear.

H: Spirit, who—who are you?

[Static noises stop. Wind rushes in. Thunder strikes in the distance.]

S: *Hannah, did you hear the thunder? My mom is going to get so mad if she finds us up here during a thunderstorm.*

H: *We can't stop now. We have to find out if there is or isn't a ghost.* Spirit, what is your name?

[Wind picks up. A branch whips against the side of the treehouse, violently. Muffled sounds of falling rain.]

S: Whoa. I don't think I'll ever get over this weird feeling. Hannah, do you feel it, too?

H: The triangle is pulling hard. I think—I think there might be a ghost.

[Loud thunder strike, and a yelp from Sam as he jumps in surprise.]

S: *Oh no! I'm sorry!*

> (Journal, Sam is apologizing because, when he jumped, the triangle launched off the board.)

H: *That's okay. I think I jumped, too! We just need to find it—fast.*

[Thud.]

S: *Ow, that was my head.*

> (Sam started to kneel and lost his balance. He hit his head against the wall.)

H: *Did you see where the triangle went?*

S: *I think it flew into the corner. One second, I brought a flashlight.*

[Click.]

S: *Oh no. It's stuck in a crack between two planks. Any sudden move could shake it loose. If it falls into the weeds, we'll never find it.*

H: Hold on, Ghost! We'll be back in a sec.

[Rain sounds intensify. The entire treehouse creaks in the wind. Crash!—a large branch hits the treehouse. The planks move. The triangle starts to fall between the crack. Thwack!—the sound of two bodies belly flopping onto the floor.]

S: *NOOoooOOOoooo! I just caught it! Do you think we can fix it?*

H: *We can try.* Listeners, what you have just heard is a minor hiccup in our investigation. Sam grabbed the triangle, but it seems to have snapped into many pieces due to Sam's extreme strength.

S: And the triangle's poor quality. I take back my shout-out for Jemma. If you're looking for quality goods, Joe is probably a better call.

H: We will try to fix this and contact our ghost again. Sam, let's do the closing ceremony. Quickly! The thunder is getting closer.

S: All right, I've sprinkled salt all over the board and grabbed the glow sticks. Thank the spirits in three . . . two . . . one . . .

H and S: Thank you, spirits!

End of recording

11
TRIPLE
THE TROUBLES

Dear Journal,

Why does trouble always come in threes?

First, the triangle cannot be fixed. The so-called magic that binds the board together seems to make the triangle resistant to all repairs: glue, tape, even pipe cleaners are not strong enough to hold the triangle together. And no matter how we arrange the parts, there's always a little chip on the bottom of it. Most likely, the fragment fell into Sam's backyard (which is a complete jungle) and will never be seen again.

This morning, I walked by Jemma's on the way to school, hoping to get some sort of replacement. Sam said a refund would be okay, but I wanted a whole new setup—a new board *and* a new triangle. I had to know whether or not Sam's ghost was real, because after the second séance, it was getting harder to say that it wasn't. I mean, the wind could have been moving the triangle, but it really did seem to be pulling our fingers this time. Then again, we might have just gotten carried away by the stormy night.

Anyway, going to Jemma's before 2:00 p.m. is always risky. Not because the store might be closed—she opens at five, an hour before Joe's—but because Jemma usually isn't too approachable until she's had her fifth cup of coffee, which she usually drinks at lunchtime. So you can imagine how pleased she was to see me when I knocked on her door at six thirty.

"Hannah Edwards. What are you doing here at this ungodly hour?" She tried to cover her hair, rolled in old-fashioned Velcro curlers, with a floppy hat.

"Hi, Jemma, I'm looking to exchange some faulty merchandise."

"Faulty merchandise? I don't sell faulty merchandise. Are you sure you didn't get it from Joe's?" Jemma chuckled at her own joke.

"Can I explain inside?" Even though it was early fall, the morning air was especially nippy.

"I suppose so." She opened the screen door and waved me in.

Jemma's shop doesn't really look like a shop. It's more like the inside of a very enthusiastic collector's house. There's an ornate glass display case in the near right corner of the living room with small porcelain figurines and two taxidermy skunks. Empty picture frames, paintings, and posters line the walls from the ceilings to the baseboards. The ceilings are used as a display for old chandeliers—there are at least five in the living room alone.

The centerpiece of the shop is Jemma's couch. Two of its cushions are covered in what Jemma affectionately calls "bits and bobs." The third cushion is where Jemma likes to sit and watch TV; its indentations and grease marks make it "well loved."

Directly in front of the couch is a table towering with books, boxes, and board games. Jemma navigated this claustrophobic mess like a professional figure skater, her hips narrowly avoiding leaning boxes, her head neatly ducking under the chandeliers, her feet gliding around various animal furs that were for sale.

"Now, where is that coffee cup? I swore I put it down here somewhere. Hannah? Have you seen my coffee cup?" I pointed to a simple blue mug on the couch's armrest.

"No, silly, that one is an antique! The one I'm looking for is about yea big, with a handle that goes like this." Although Jemma's hand movements were supposed to be helpful, the mug she described did not exist on this planet. (Unless someone has seen a foot-wide mug with a four-pronged handle.) Nevertheless, I was hunting for Jemma's mythical mug, lifting various rugs, looking behind boxes, trying not to break anything, when she erupted into sudden shouts of "Don't touch that!" After ten minutes, we abandoned our search, and I attempted to negotiate with two-coffee Jemma.

"So, Jemma, about my exchange . . . Sam said he got this board from you four days ago, and he would have come here himself, but he was getting ready for swim practice. The main triangle piece shattered. Do you possibly have a new box set—or even a replacement triangle? It's kind of urgent."

"Let me take a look at that." Jemma took the box from my hands, shaking it slightly. She opened it up, inspecting each piece by bringing it within a millimeter of her eye. As she reached the triangle, she started to cluck (yes, cluck). "This piece looks like it has been tampered with."

"Um, we tried to fix it after it broke."

"And how did it break?"

"Well, we were conducting a séance, and it slipped out of our hands, and when we grabbed it, it shattered."

"A séance, huh? The piece shattering is not a good sign. Not a good sign at all."

"What do you mean?"

"There's a chance that whatever you summoned was too powerful for the board's magic. You see, this board is only designed to help you"—she read the box—"'summon the dead, speak to your long-lost relatives, and have ghost-loads of spooky fun with your friends.' It's not equipped to handle powerful spirits. If you ask me, you and Sam encountered an angry spirit, one that could even be evil."

"It didn't seem very evil." I suspected that Jemma was trying to avoid replacing the board by suggesting we had misused it. "In fact, the spirit barely said anything."

"Did you experience any cold spots? Changing weather conditions? Feelings of impending doom?"

"Well, the first night was chilly, and then the second time there was a thunderstorm, but surely—" Jemma's gasp cut off my explanation.

"Those are all signs of a dark spirit. You should be very careful, Hannah." She handed the board back to me. "Now, as far as an exchange, as you can see on the board, it is a 'One-of-a-Kind Supernatural Device.' I don't have any others."

"Isn't that just some marketing gimmick?" I asked, and Jemma gasped again.

"Hannah Edwards, nothing that I sell is a gimmick! I only sell *real* antiques and curiosities. Real and *rare* ones."

"Well, can you at least try to replace the broken part?"

"Sadly not. And I cannot process a monetary return as this board has been used, tainted with evil energy, and tampering with any part voids the warranty. Can I interest you in something else? A crystal ball, perhaps?" Jemma held up a small ball that I had previously thought was a candleholder.

"Or how about this doodad? You might be able to

video your ghost." Now, she held up a video camera that looked like it had been created in the Stone Age. I really wanted another Ouija board, but a camera might come in handy.

"I'll take the camera."

Jemma smiled warmly. "Wonderful. One camera in exchange for the remains of the board." She pasted an orange sticker on the back of the camera—that's her system of receipts. Orange means final sale. She held the door open for me, loudly proclaiming, "Pleasure doing business with you. Do come again!"

"Quiet down. You don't need to announce *every* sale!" Joe called out from next door. I rushed away—Jemma and Joe's arguments are legendary, and I did *not* want to get caught between them.

Trouble number two was much worse than what happened at Jemma's. At lunch, Sam and I were brainstorming new ways to contact the ghost when a syrupy voice radiated from the overhead speakers in the cafeteria: "Hannah Edwards, please report to Ms. Grant after school today."

The chess club seeing me leave her office was bad enough—now the entire school knew! It felt as though every head turned my way, all voices reduced to a solemn hush, and every person in every grade knew who I was and that I had done something wrong. Sam insisted that I was exaggerating. He said most kids were too busy eating lunch to notice. But he didn't understand the threat of being found out—of having other kids know that you're not normal. He didn't know how much work I'd put into seeming "right" and how Ms. Grant's announcement could strip that work away.

Whether or not they heard or cared, Ms. Grant's announcement was still a deliberate attack. She wanted to humiliate me. The question was, Why?

"Maybe it's just a check-in," Sam reassured me, but his attempt to comfort me did little to shrink my anger and embarrassment.

And now the third trouble: actually facing Ms. Grant after school. As I walked up to her office, I stomped extra hard, hoping to make the door vibrate, to make it shed pounds of glitter.

I stared at the cat posters with defiance. Only yesterday, I had run away from this door, vowing never to return, and yet here I was, dragged back to the dungeon against my will. This time, however, was different. I was so angry that I could probably have breathed fire, too. I knocked on the door and imagined I was a knight using a battering ram to break into the dragon's castle. Are fire-breathing knights a thing?

As I was mentally rehearsing my forceful—yet witty—greeting, Ms. Grant swung open the door, and my nostrils were stung by the sadly familiar smell of pumpkin spice.

"Hannah! I'm so glad you're here. Come in, come in. How have you been? I hope you didn't mind the announcement, but you seemed so *jumpy* about me meeting you at your locker, and I didn't want to frighten you. Have you been using your tools?"

Ms. Grant's onslaught of questions buried all my witty responses. I had to settle for a pathetic "No, I have not had a chance to use the tools yet" as I looked for an appropriate cushion. My green-haired nemesis had migrated across the room. Even though it could have been moved by another student, I preferred to imagine it had sprouted legs and crawled around at night.

"Oh, Hannah, I know that, as a student, you are busy, but trust me, you're just going to get busier. One day, you'll think back and say, 'Look at all the time I had!' And you'll wish that you had begun the healing process earlier. These tools are useful life skills that will help you evolve into a fully equipped adult. You know, I wish I had had that meditation exercise when *I* was your age. If I had started practicing mindfulness then, why, who *knows* what I could have become!" Ms. Grant threw her hands up in the air, a gesture that was meant to suggest endless possibilities but instead made it look like she was trying very hard to sprout wings. "Either way, Hannah, I don't want to scold you. I'm not in the scolding business. I'm in the helping business. So, what have you gotten up to recently? Anything big?" She folded herself into a position that could only be comfortable for a praying mantis.

"Nothing comes to mind." Unlike Jemma, who actually believes in "the occult," Ms. Grant strikes me as the type who would write off my séances as "superstitious delusions" or a medical issue. Even if she did believe me, I didn't want her to be the first to hear about our ghost research.

"Last year you were on the soccer team. Are you doing that again this year?"

With all that had been going on, soccer was the last thing on my mind. I hadn't even bothered to go to tryouts. "Not this year. Maybe next year!"

"Hmmmm. 'Next year' is a dangerous attitude. You don't want to live your life putting off the life that you want to live! That wouldn't be living!" I'd heard that dragons liked to tell riddles. This wasn't exactly a riddle, but it was close.

"On the other hand," Ms. Grant went on, "it can be *very good* to deliberately take a restful break. Are you doing any extracurriculars?"

Ms. Grant's curious stare bothered me. As a counselor, she had access to all my records—including any extracurriculars I'd signed up for this semester. I could feel a bit of fire in my voice as I responded, "As you likely know, I have not signed up for any extracurriculars this semester.

Why are you asking? Are you recruiting for a club?" I tried to make the last question sound innocent, not snotty. I clearly failed.

"I am just trying to get to know you, Hannah. You see, your teachers and I get to see you on the surface—we know some things about you, we get some idea about your out-of-school life, but we never see *the real you*. As a counselor, it is my job to look deeper and figure out *why* you are acting a certain way. I'm not your enemy."

For a moment, a fleeting moment, Ms. Grant did not seem like a dragon. She seemed like a person trying to do her job, an exhausting job that involved getting an irritable kid to trust her.

Any sympathy that I was feeling evaporated as Ms. Grant spoke again, this time in a pitch that could only be heard by small dogs and children. "In any event, I did not call you into my office to invite you to join a special *club*. I called you in because *we* are concerned about some recent erratic behavior. Now, during our last session, I mentioned that I was trying to create a guide—a how-to—to cope with your recent loss. This is a standard technique when we are dealing with students who are experiencing grief—a hands-off approach. But if a student starts to show changed behavior—if the how-to guide isn't working—then we might need a more hands-on approach.

"As I've already noted, you were previously *very*

engaged in extracurriculars. Yet now you have not registered for a single one. Furthermore, not just one but *several* teachers have observed some odd behaviors. Before our first meeting, I spoke to your teachers and learned that you were passing notes in Ms. Luna's class, something you don't usually do. And Ms. Knugen noticed that you were inattentive. And now, Mr. Lewis saw you hiding underneath a tree—alone.

"As I'm sure you *know*, these are all very *minor* incidents when taken one at a time. But my job isn't to think one at a time. It's to look at the bigger picture. And these incidents all suggest that something *big* is changing below the surface—that something is bubbling up. Especially given the newest development."

The newest development?

"You may ask yourself, 'What is the newest development?'"

Ms. Grant got that one right.

"Well, Hannah, you're a bright girl. Do you have any ideas?"

I shook my head.

"Hannah, do you know when your book report for Ms. Luna's class was due?" Ms. Grant leaned forward. Although her tone was sympathetic, her eyes revealed a secret glee at my discomfort. I realized my mistake: Up until this point, I had been thinking that she was the dragon, and

I was the hero. But, in Ms. Grant's eyes, I was the dragon, and she was just about to slay me.

My voice, embarrassingly, trembled as I whispered, "Next Friday, Ginger." As I said her first name, Ms. Grant's face burst into a sharp-toothed smile.

"Now that's more like it!" She immediately hid her grin beneath a mask of authority. "However, Hannah, Ms. Luna's book report was due yesterday."

That was the death blow. I was slain. I hoped that I would make a nicer cushion than the green creature. There was no need to say, "You're wrong, Ms. Grant!" No need to fight back. Because, as Ms. Grant spoke, I realized that she was completely right. I could clearly remember the whiteboard marker squeaking as Ms. Luna underlined "Due: September 12" in red. How could I have let it slip my mind? Why didn't I start it earlier? Then I could have handed something in now! I hadn't even read the book yet. I was—I am—so stupid! Especially since Mom had reminded me about it. I had done *something wrong*. Even though I *knew* that handing in one project late wasn't a big deal, it felt like some major part of myself had been wiped away. Before I was Hannah Edwards: good student, good community member, punctual. Now I was Hannah Edwards: decent student, good community member, missed an assignment—probably something secretly wrong with her.

I must have stayed in Ms. Grant's office for another

fifteen minutes. I must have responded to her questions. Snippets of words formed in the orange fog. I remember her saying something about how "Ms. Luna would have talked to you personally, but, because of your father's recent disappearance, I figured it was better that I talk to you. As you know, I am a qualified counselor." (Does somebody need to be "qualified" to talk to me?)

"Since this is the first deadline you've missed in her class, it isn't a big deal." (Not a big deal? It changed everything! My eyes drifted over to the green cushion. I think it called me "failure"—or was that Ms. Grant? Or was it just in my head?)

"Nobody needs to know. Not your mom, not your friends, not even any other teachers! It can be our little secret." (I guess I was the type of kid who needed to keep secrets with Ms. Grant.)

"Have you done any work on the project so far?"

I shook my head no. Even though I knew I should have been working in advance—three days isn't enough to write a good book report.

"That's okay! You've just got to put pen to paper, as they say. Here's the deal: Since you thought the report was due next Friday, I'm sure that you've budgeted time for it. Why not just work on your planned schedule and hand it in on Friday? I will talk to Ms. Luna, and it will be like this never happened."

How could I describe that I couldn't work on that schedule anymore? Working on a project before it's due is one thing. I've never worked on a late project before. Which was a whole different kind of pressure. Yes, I know that lateness shouldn't affect the difficulty in writing. But it still made me want to puke.

"I will try my best. Thank you for your understanding." Every word that came out of my mouth felt like it was from some greeting card.

"I'm so *glad* to hear that, Hannah! And if you start to feel overwhelmed, remember your tool kit! And there are some other things that can help you feel less distracted. First of all, I would recommend no video games—those will just make you more hyper. Second, try using a planner! Maybe even take away TV if you miss a goal. It might seem harsh, but these are good first steps for getting back on track. . . ."

The green creature's fur was forming an evil grin. This was what I deserved for sitting on it yesterday. Besides, it had been an A student once, but then it had become a *BAD KID* and sprouted green fur. How much longer before I got green fur?

"Okay. I think we understand each other. Remember: It'll be our little secret. Just don't let it happen again."

I didn't want to know what would happen to me if I did let it happen again. Also, I wanted to tell her that I didn't *let* "it" happen in the first place. That since I couldn't prevent "it" from happening the first time, I might not be able to stop "it" from happening again.

But I didn't voice these thoughts because I knew that Ms. Grant was right. That, for most people, refocusing shouldn't be a big deal—and for the miraculous Hannah Edwards, it *definitely* shouldn't be a big deal. And telling her that I couldn't do it because my brain wanted to be someplace else didn't feel right. She was already pulling some strings for me. Maybe she wasn't an evil, knight-eating dragon but one of those friendly ones who was just trying to protect the princess.

"I think that we have made a *lot* of big progress in this session! Now, we don't want to lose that progress, do we?" I nodded without fully realizing what I was agreeing to. My chest felt heavy and hollow at the same time.

"Fantastic! I am so *glad* that you agree. I think that a reasonable schedule—at least until you've finished your report—is to quickly check in with me after school every day. I will see you Monday!"

Ms. Grant, oblivious to the fact that I was now an empty shell, whipped out a pink glitter pen and a purple furry notebook from thin air. Holding the pen's cap in her mouth, she wrote something down. She looked at me from under her eyelashes and smiled. "Do you want me to give you a sticky note as a reminder?"

"No, thank you." I was surprised when I spoke. No part of me had decided to say those words. It was like my body was speaking, not my brain.

"Well, on second thought, since you have been a little bit forgetful lately, I'll give you one just in case." A stack of green sticky notes appeared in her hand. She grabbed a purple glitter pen, wrote something, ripped the note from the stack, and handed it to me. I've put it here:

> APPOINTMENT WITH GINGER
> MONDAY AT 3:00 P.M.

"Off you go, Hannah!" she chirped. Even though, mere seconds ago, I could not wait to leave Ms. Grant's lair, I couldn't move at all. The orange had finally paralyzed me. I was aware of every single step it took to stand: Get your feet under your legs, then push up through your toes. Then push up with your hands, lifting your shoulders. That's it. Now stand.

Ms. Grant watched my struggle with fascination. Once I was steady, I pushed my slumped body toward the door. "Hannah, honey." Ms. Grant giggled. "Don't forget your bag! You really need to pay attention to these things. What would you have done if you'd gotten home without your homework?"

In a rare moment of generosity, she scooped up my backpack and brought it to me. As she reached for the doorknob to let me out, I noticed a line of dark brown makeup dividing her face from her neck. *That's the zipper for her human mask*, I thought.

She bared her teeth in what was meant to be a smile. "What would you do without me?" She sighed, lightly tapping my head. I shuddered. "Off you go, then! See you soon!"

I wanted to run home, but I lost all my steam the second I caught a breath of fresh air. Usually, when I stayed late after school, Dad would pick me up on his way home from work. It wasn't a long drive, but he said that it was more fun to have a copilot. In the winter, when it got dark early, he told me he would lose his way if I wasn't there to guide him. I wondered if Dad didn't come home the night he went missing because I wasn't there to be his copilot, and I couldn't get that thought out of my head as I walked home alone and went upstairs to write all this down, Journal.

I guess trouble doesn't come in threes. It comes in fours: Now I have to see Ms. Grant on Monday.

Actually, scratch that. I just heard Uncle Fergus's sports car pull into the driveway. Trouble clearly comes in fives.

12
COWBOY HATS AND CUTTING CLASS

Dinner with Fergus was surprisingly pleasant compared to the meeting with Ms. Grant. His ludicrous stories were a welcome distraction from the deadline that hovered over my head. The only annoyance was Fergus's newfound desire to ask me questions about myself.

"So, Hannah, have you decided to rejoin the soccer team this year? You know, I heard they are looking for a new coach. Maybe I could sign up! Wouldn't that be fun?"

"I don't think I'm going to do soccer this year." His questions reminded me of Ms. Grant's unrelenting campaign.

"Oh, that's a pity. Sports are a great way to grow self-discipline—that means self-control. A way of being a better you."

My heart skipped a beat. Why did Fergus suddenly think I needed to be a better me? Had I slipped up somehow? Had he seen me zoning out?

No, I thought. *Stay calm. He couldn't have noticed anything.*

"But if soccer isn't your thing," he went on, "maybe there's something else. You know, your father and I were on the field hockey team together. I know, I know, it's not as *cool* as soccer, but it's a very tough sport!"

I nodded in agreement.

"Speaking of which, that's how your father got his first cowboy hat. It was a prize for scoring the game-winning goal. Even though *I* was actually responsible for the win because I blocked a record number of goals. But hey, ever since then, your dad always wore a cowboy hat. They don't make hats better than the one he wore. I sure have been thinking about that hat lately. What with him missing and all. You haven't happened to see it—have you?"

Fergus's eyebrows danced like two fuzzy caterpillars as he spoke. I, for one, was lost in the image of Dad scoring the winning goal. He really was—is—the town's hero. I hated hearing Fergus talk about him like some long-gone Western celebrity—like Wallace Morrow. I looked over at Mom, who was smiling at Fergus. Here he was, another man sitting in Dad's seat, and it was like she didn't even notice the difference. And now he wanted Dad's hat.

"Earth to Hannah? I asked you a question."

"Oh, I haven't seen it." I looked down at my plate. Overcooked chicken tonight. Yummy.

"You give me a holler if you do. But don't go out of your way looking for anything. That's the sheriff's job." Fergus sawed through the piece of bone-dry chicken on his plate.

"Oh, by the way, Barbara," he said, his teeth taking up the chicken challenge now, "have you had a chance to look at those papers yet?"

"Not yet."

"Well, I know you're busy, but it would be helpful if you gave them a look when you have the time. It'll really help me get the ball rolling on the farm."

"I'll try to get them to you as soon as possible," Mom said.

She and Fergus continued to chat, completely ignorant of the falling feeling in my stomach. To them, things seemed back to normal. Discussing papers, exchanging childhood stories, laughing at jokes. Meanwhile, all I could think about was how Dad would have told the field hockey story better than Fergus. How he used to oversee all the things on the farm. How his shadow was much bigger than Fergus's. How Fergus kept rocking back on his chair, which Dad hated. How, when Dad cooked chicken, it was moist because he put a can of soda in its butt. Without him, the air in the room seemed stale. Everything was totally off. The only thing keeping me from sinking down into my chair entirely was the thought that I'd find him soon.

By the time I went to bed, the meeting with Ms. Grant felt like ages ago, and writing the book report no longer felt like an impossible task. It felt so achievable, in fact, that I decided to start on it over the weekend, when I would be in a fresher state of mind.

That, as it turned out, was a terrible idea. On Saturday, the simple five-page book report morphed in my mind into a fifteen-foot-tall, big red deadline, and I panicked. I decided to put the paper off again until Monday after school, when I would feel calmer. As I made breakfast Monday morning, the sound of cereal hitting the bowl reminded me of Ms. Grant's clacking fingernails and our upcoming appointment. And that made me realize I had even less time in the afternoon than I had thought!

The walk to school was unbearable. Every kind look, every familiar smile, every gentle call-out from a teacher now felt like a miniature interrogation—an attempt to catch some ripple that indicated a "bigger issue." Suddenly, it felt like everyone could see the real me—the one I thought I had been hiding so successfully. But half the things the teachers had reported as possible problems with my behavior weren't even a big deal. So what if I sat under the pine tree? Mr. Lewis must have seen me after Sam and Tim had left.

I stood before the school fence, staring up at the posts. It looked more like a prison than ever before. I was now being watched—in a land controlled by a dragon who brainwashed teachers into spying for her, who was trying to find new problems and twisting the ones that existed.

If I had attracted Ms. Grant's poisonous gaze by being the victim of a tragedy, then the only solution was to erase that tragedy: I had to find my dad.

But finding time to investigate was getting harder to do. I had to work on that book report. I had to meet with Ms. Grant. I had a math assignment to complete and science homework, too. I had to go to class and pretend to pay attention so no one would worry about me. Or discover the secret about the real me. Every task seemed equally important, like if each wasn't done *right now* then it could never get done. And whenever I decided on one task to finish, the others called out, "HEY, WHAT ABOUT ME!" It felt like my brain was spinning in circles even though I was standing still.

So I did what usually helps when I need to hit reset.

I decided to take a walk.

My watch beeped, reminding me I had five minutes before class—I set timers sometimes so I'm not late—but I shut it off and wandered toward the forest. I don't know why I headed there. My feet seemed to be leading me without consulting my brain. As if an invisible force had control over my legs.

And before I realized where I was headed, I was standing in front of the Old Grain Mill.

Even though I've walked by the mill plenty of times, I've never gone inside it. Mainly because old, abandoned places are creepy.

For kids, old places are scary because we're afraid of rats or spiders or skeletons. Adults find old places scary for entirely different reasons. They see rotting foundations and loose wires and rusted metal. Nevertheless, these places are usually only scary when it's dark out. That's when the rats leave their nests, the spiders slip down from their webs, and stepping on a shard of glass or a rusty nail is a real possibility.

But the Old Grain Mill was well lit. Light shone through the two dusty windows and down from a hole in the roof. I peered through the doorway. Because the sun was directly overhead, there were no spooky shadows that you could mistake for a monster.

I saw four sacks of something in the far left corner, sitting on the floor, which was pressed dirt. There were empty soda cans in the far right corner and some candy wrappers scattered throughout the room, probably dumped by teenagers.

There was nothing the least bit scary here—until I walked inside.

The minute I entered, the air turned chilly. And I could see my breath. And the windows slowly iced over with layers of frost.

And I met Sam's ghost.

13
GHOST
RULES AND TRICKS

Jemma had warned me about evil spirits, but the faintly glowing figure didn't seem threatening. Crouched in the dimmest corner of the room, he didn't make any move to attack me. But the very fact that he was there, pale, translucent, and shimmering, was more terrifying than anything I could have ever imagined.

Sam's description of his encounter with the ghost now seemed far too straightforward. Why didn't he mention the feeling of being in a dream even though you knew you were awake?

When Sam and I had held our séances, I always doubted the existence of the ghost. I truly believed we were moving the triangle, especially that last time, because anyone could get caught up in the ritual, sitting in the dark, high up in the tree with the wind and rain making things scarier.

But there was no denying this shimmering figure.

For a moment, the ghost and I silently observed each other. Or I think it was observing me.

I continued to stare at the creature in shock and surprise. It was filmy, and its features were blurry. There was no way to tell who it might be. But I kept trying. I stared so hard and so long, I was beginning to feel cross-eyed. I forced myself to take a deep breath.

I finally gathered my courage and spoke, trying to steady the tremor in my voice. "Hello? Wh-who are you?"

There was a moment of heart-pounding silence. Something above me creaked. The wind whistled through a crack in the planks. Outside, a car skidded over some gravel. I remembered that the ghost didn't speak to Sam. I wished I had brought the Ouija board. Maybe the ghost could have guided my fingers, pointing to letters to spell things out. As I thought about this, a deep voice cut through the air.

"Hannah, it's me. Your father."

Every muscle in my body tensed. There was no way this ghost was my father. Its scratchy voice didn't sound like him. And other than being vaguely human-shaped, it didn't look anything like him. This creature, huddled in a corner, appeared smaller than my dad. It could have been anybody.

Maybe there really is an Old Mill Ghost, I thought,

and he's pretending to be my dad. "You don't look like my father," I said.

The ghost's head turned down, inspecting its translucent arms and legs. "When I'm out too long during the day, I begin to lose my shape. Do you remember that book about ghosts I gave you on your ninth birthday?"

Wait. How did he know about that book?

I started to feel lightheaded.

I took a deep breath.

This is the Old Mill Ghost, trying to trick me. Ghosts can find out all sorts of things, I reminded myself. *There were lots of people at my ninth birthday party, and I carried that book around for weeks. The whole town knew about it. The ghost could have found out about it from any one of them.*

"I remember the book that *my dad* gave me on my ninth birthday," I said.

"Well, that book got some stuff about ghosts right and a lot of stuff wrong. Do you remember all the blurry ghost pictures?" Unlike Ms. Grant, the ghost paused after every question, giving me time to answer.

"Yes."

"We used to joke that they needed better cameras. But now that I'm a ghost, I know the truth. Those blurred figures are what ghosts turn into after a while.

"You see, during the night, ghosts can materialize anywhere they want, so long as they have been there before. Nighttime is a lot of fun for ghosts. Since we can slip through walls, moving around is easy. We can check out museums, sneak into movies—anything you can imagine. Really!

"But if we stay out too long during the day, we start to lose our shape. We can restore it, but that takes a lot of energy. And ghosts are short on energy. So each time we transform back, there's a price to pay—we lose a memory.

"Some ghosts have re-formed so many times, they've used up all their memories. They've forgotten their family and friends. Their names. Their homes. Eventually, they forget what they looked like, so they couldn't restore themselves even if they had the energy to do it. In the end, they make new homes in treasure chests, dark corners, and closets without a clue about who they were, where they came from, and where they belong."

As the ghost spoke, my skin chilled. *This can't be happening*, I thought. Except that it was. I was looking right at a ghost, and I was talking to it. I couldn't help but ask, "Do ghosts stay here forever?"

"Some do. But they have to remember not to go out during the day. The ones who forget . . . well . . . they float out into the sunlight one too many times, and poof—they're gone."

"Gone where?"

The ghost shuddered. "I don't know. None of us do. I learned about losing my form the hard way. I went out too many times during the day. That's probably why you don't recognize me. But I don't want to re-form. I can't risk losing any memories. They are too important. I have a problem to solve here, and I need to remember it. I need to save my strength. And I need your help."

My dad always said the more complicated a person's story, the more likely they were lying. The best strategy is just to tell the simple, straightforward truth. Something about the ghost's story wasn't adding up. And I wasn't about to help it until it did. "Okay, but how do I know that you're not the Old Mill Ghost? And why didn't you tell Sam who you were?"

"I remember seeing Sam! I tried to talk to him, but he couldn't hear me. That's when I learned that ghosts can only talk to their own blood relatives. It's because our spirits are connected."

This ghost was very convincing, but there were still things that didn't make sense. "Why haven't you tried to talk to me before this? Why didn't you show up at home? Why did you wait four months?"

"I had to save my energy. I was trying to solve my problem, and I needed to make sure I didn't disappear before I did."

"Okay, let's say, hypothetically, that I believe you

about all this ghost stuff. You still haven't proven that you're my father. Tell me one thing that only my dad would know."

"I can tell you lots of things. I know that on your fifth birthday you decided you were an archaeologist, and you dug up everything in the backyard. I know that your favorite animals are frogs, and when you were seven you filled up the pool with tadpoles to create a frog army. I know that you never liked squash—even as a baby."

Journal, I have to admit it—my heart started to race. These things were all true. I wanted this ghost to stop talking. I didn't want it to be my father.

"I know that you like to read for thirty minutes before bedtime, and after your mom shuts off the light, you turn on a flashlight and keep reading under your covers." The ghost finally paused. "Do you want to hear any more? I'm your father, Hannah, and I love you. I could talk about you all day."

I turned away from the ghost as it said those last words. I suddenly remembered something that made me feel less panicky. Even though the ghost knew all these things, it didn't mean the ghost was my dad.

The ghost book I had gotten for my ninth birthday had an entire chapter on why you should never trust a ghost. Sometimes they aren't who they claim to be. Some ghosts lead people into marshes and make them get lost, just for fun! Others are not actually ghosts, but demons in disguise, trying to convince you to do bad stuff.

But basically, you can never judge a ghost by its cover story. Plus, it's been said that the Old Mill Ghost is notoriously mischievous. It could have been watching our family for years.

And I couldn't forget Jemma's warning about dark spirits.

All of this meant that this ghost didn't have to be—that it wasn't—my dad. My dad was still alive. Just missing.

The ghost interrupted my thoughts. "Hannah, do you believe me now? We don't have much time. I have something very important to tell you. It's so important that I'd rather not burden you with it. That's one of the reasons it's taken me all this time to talk to you. I wish somebody else could help me, but you're the only one who can."

My dad taught me lots of things, and one was that people who are up to no good will create a "false sense of urgency"—a feeling that something has to be done *right this second* or else the world will cave in. The elaborate story, the book of ghosts, the final "important" mission—they all made me suspicious about this ghost. Very suspicious.

"I have to go. I'm late for school." I started for the door.

"Hannah, wait!" it shouted, but I kept on going.

When I reached the door, I turned back, half-expecting to see the ghost transforming into some terrifying creature, revealing its true self. Instead, I saw it fading into the shadows—growing fainter and fainter, until it disappeared.

14
THE
LATE PASS

Wubpa wubpa wubpa wubpa. That's the sound that the laminated late pass made as Ms. Grant fanned herself with it.

She had given it to me this morning because I was a half hour late to school. Usually you need a note from a parent to get a late pass, but Ms. Grant said she'd make an exception. She'd given me the pass *and* she wouldn't tell my mother as long as I told her where I'd been this morning.

It was afternoon now, and here I was in her office. I returned the pass and watched her cool herself with it as though she were trying to ward off a fainting fit.

"Hannah, needless to say, I am *very* concerned. You seemed so motivated after our last meeting! You know, I am here to help and support you. *Clearly,* I must be doing something wrong since your behavior is only getting worse."

Usually, Ms. Grant's combination of concern and false modesty would have gotten under my skin, but after meeting with an actual ghost, being late didn't feel very important. For today—just today—I'd have to give myself a break for not being perfect.

Plus, Journal, I have to admit, Ms. Grant was right about my behavior—and she didn't even know it. I barely paid attention in class today. I'd seen a real ghost, and I couldn't stop thinking about it. Sam was out sick, so I couldn't talk to him about it, but I had to be right—that ghost was the Old Mill Ghost, trying to trick me. Instead of taking notes in English, I made this list:

Why the Ghost Was NOT My Dad
1. It didn't look like my dad.
2. Ghosts lie about who they are.
3. The Old Mill Ghost had years to learn all about us.
4. If the ghost really was my dad, it wouldn't have waited four months to find me. It would have looked for me right away, no matter how much ghost energy it used.
5. The ghost is not Dad because my dad is not dead.

Anyway, back to Ms. Grant, who kept going on and on. . . .

"Here I am, really sticking my neck out for you, really trying to help you, but, Hannah, it doesn't feel like you *want* my help. Am I correct in making that assumption?" she asked.

"No, Ms. Grant—I mean Ginger. I appreciate your help. I'm not trying to get you in trouble. I just have other things on my mind," I said.

Ms. Grant stopped waving the pass in the air and neatly placed it on her lap. Today, her drawn-on eyebrows were slightly lopsided, so I couldn't tell whether she was raising one when she uttered a deep, echoing, "Ooooh."

"You know, Hannah, this is a *safe space*, a space where you are free to express yourself. This is the perfect place to tell me what exactly is on your mind. Does it have anything to do with why you were late today or your father's disappearance?"

Outside, I could hear kids playing, not soccer, maybe . . . softball? The dull thud of a ball hitting a bat confirmed it. Sam's probably told me a thousand times: Softball has an *underhand* pitch and a bigger ball. The coach whistled three times. I wondered what that meant. I should have been out there playing, not stuck inside being interrogated, especially because there was a logical explanation for my behavior.

There was only one way to get out of this prison: I needed to prove to Ms. Grant that there wasn't anything bad going on, that I was just working on a bigger project, and once everything was done, I'd be back to my normal self (I hoped).

"In some ways, it does," I said. Ms. Grant motioned for me to continue. "Everything here is confidential, right?"

"Of course! As I said on the first day, I'm just a big, friendly safe. I'm here to help!" Ms. Grant's grin reminded me of a documentary I watched on monkeys: When monkeys smile, they aren't trying to be friendly. They are warning their prey that they are about to bite them.

"Okay. Well, just between us, you are right. I've been concentrating on my dad. But not in the way that you might think. It's not just that I miss him. I'm taking action and looking into his disappearance. That's why I missed the deadline. And that's why I was late this morning. I was, um, following a lead."

As soon as I said that, I realized I'd made a mistake. I definitely did not want to talk about the ghost with Ms. Grant.

"What type of lead?" Ms. Grant asked.

I knew it. I knew I shouldn't have said that. Still, I thought starting with that question was kind of strange. Where was the lecture about leaving things to the authorities? Where was the explanation about different ways of "processing" and "handling" grief?

"I was just walking through town. Retracing his steps. Hoping to pick up his trail before it turned cold," I lied.

"Thank you for sharing that information with me, Hannah. I understand your desire to get your father back home, safe and sound. But four months is a long time. If there was a trail with clues, I'm sure they would have all blown away by now. So how about you concentrate on your school assignments? You don't want to fall too far behind."

Once again, Ms. Grant's reply caught me by surprise. She was acting so reasonable . . . so nice.

Maybe it was because she thought she was winning—that I had finally "opened up." Maybe a dragon isn't a dragon when it gets what it wants. Or maybe Ms. Grant wasn't really all that bad. Maybe she was only an enemy because that's how I saw her.

Or maybe there was something else behind it. Because she reached under a pile of papers on her desk and made some notes. I almost didn't think anything of it, until a glimmer of gold caught my eye. The paper she was writing on had a golden canola plant embossed on the top. Just like my dad's business stationery. When she saw me staring at it, she quickly slipped it into the top drawer of the file cabinet and locked it away. She pulled on the handle just to make sure it was shut tight.

Was it my dad's stationery? And if it was, why did she have it?

"Now, here's another *really* useful tool for you, Hannah!" she went on. "Tonight, I want you to go home and write a list of ten things you like about yourself! And don't forget the calming exercise."

Journal, it took me all evening to record today's events. And I couldn't stop thinking about that stationery. But I made the list Ms. Grant asked for, and I attached it below. The task was hard to take seriously. I guess the book report will have to wait until tomorrow.

Ten Things I Like About Myself

1. Fun
2. Smart
3. Hardworking
4. Talented
5. Helpful
6. Open-minded
7. Logical
8. Good at climbing trees
9. A Friend of the Frogs
10. Soft and saggy

15
TREASURE, BETRAYAL, AND THE TRUTH

The thing people don't tell you about cutting class is once you've done it, boy, is it ever easy to do again.

I resisted the temptation for a while, until today. As I entered Ms. Luna's class, she announced we were going to review sentence structure. Review it? Why did we have to review it? We just learned it—at an unbearably slow pace, I might add. Without learning any new material, my mind would spin and spin and overthink and fixate on the ghost. I wanted to talk to it to find out how it knew all those things about me. And the ghost said it had something to tell me—now I wanted to know what it was. (I tried to talk to Sam about all this last night. Get his opinion even though we don't agree all the time. But his mother said he was still not feeling well and he was sleeping. She offered to give him a message, but I couldn't exactly tell her that I'd seen a ghost. What would she think of me then?)

After class, I would have to go to Ms. Grant's and then straight home to work on my paper. And since my perfect reputation was stained anyway and could never be perfect again, I figured it was better to skip the boring review and try to get the answers I needed from the ghost.

Okay, Journal, to be honest, I think I knew that I was going to cut class no matter what and look for the ghost. This morning, right when I was about to run out the door, I was overcome by an urge to grab Dad's tape recorder—that way I could record the ghost and play it back for Sam. The moment class started, I asked to go to the bathroom, grabbed my backpack, and headed off to the mill. Even if cutting class wasn't *GOOD KID* behavior, in this case, I was convinced it was the right thing to do.

But I hadn't considered the possibility that the ghost wouldn't show up.

Journal, I've been sitting in the mill for what feels like hours now, so I decided to start on this entry. I've checked all the dark corners, under all the sacks, and even inside some cans—maybe ghosts can shrink?—and I still haven't seen any sign of it.

What if it spent too much time in the sun and can't regain its shape? What if it disappeared forever? What if I imagined it?

Journal, I don't want to think about *that*, so I'll look around and study the mill instead. The north wall is covered in scratches. Are they human scratches or did a rat make them? They don't look like rat scratches. Was a kid once trapped here in a blizzard for days and days, clawing at the wood, trying to break out? Forced to eat . . . rats?

I shouldn't have written that. Nobody is better at scaring you than yourself—you know exactly what you're afraid of.

I'm shivering now. Is it because I did such a good job frightening myself, or is it because it's getting cold in here?

Wait. I think the wall just moved. Or it seems like it did. No, that isn't the wall moving. It's something taking shape.

I'm shivering harder.

I know I came here to see the ghost, but that doesn't mean I'm not afraid. If you know anything about ghosts, Journal, know this. They are *very* unpredictable.

The shape is translucent. It seems to be stretching, as though it just woke up from a nap. I'm going to stop writing now and switch on Dad's tape recorder, Journal, so I don't miss a thing.

[Yawning.]

Ghost: Hannah? Is that you? You've come back!

Me: I had to. I need to know what you want from me. You

are not my father. My dad isn't dead. He's just missing. But you said you had something important to tell me.

(The ghost paused. Maybe it was planning how to trick me.)

Ghost: Hannah, you and your mother are in grave danger.

Me: Grave danger? Is that some kind of ghost joke?

Ghost: No. It is not a joke. Grave danger from the man responsible for my death. It's my brother. Your uncle Fergus.

Me: Uncle Fergus? Uncle Fergus is responsible for your death? How is that possible? He seems like such a clown.

Ghost: Fergus is not what he seems. His advice, his desire to help, is all a mask. He's a snake, ready to strike. I've always known this about him. Known that deep down inside, he was jealous that I'd inherited the family farm. But I didn't realize how much his jealousy had changed him. I didn't realize how far he'd go to compete with me. To prove he's better than I am. You have to believe me.

(Journal, the moment he brought up Fergus's jealousy, something seemed to fall into place. I thought about Fergus's constant bragging. About his comment that he actually was the one who saved the big game. I thought about him always coming over. Sitting in Dad's chair.

Trying to take over Dad's life. And there was something about the ghost's voice that now sounded and felt familiar. The patterns. The way the pitch went down at the end of every sentence. I read once that a voice was like a fingerprint—everybody's was completely unique.

I didn't want to believe it.

But this ghost—I think this ghost IS my dad.

My heart clenched and my breath stopped. And I suddenly felt lonely. Really lonely. And empty.

And, to be honest, maybe a bit relieved that one part of the mystery was solved.

Then I felt guilty for feeling relieved. But some part of me knew. Even before Sam told me about the ghost. I think I knew after a couple of weeks, when the county police didn't bring Dad home. The day the first casserole arrived on our porch, I think I felt some shift in the universe. I knew that day he was never coming back. So now I had to finish the puzzle. I had to find out what happened to him.)

Me: Dad, I—I believe you. How—how did you die?

(My voice sounded weird and warbly, and it came out very high-pitched.)

Dad: The day I went missing, I was on my way to meet you with a surprise—an inflatable donut raft! I was planning on rafting down the river with you, just like I did with my mom when I was a boy, and I was so excited! Now, I know the river is usually too low to use rafts, but since it was spring, I figured the runoff from the melting snow would raise the water level just enough. But as I passed over the bridge and looked down, I noticed that the level hadn't gone up. It was actually lower than before. That didn't make sense. And it wasn't just an issue for our rafting. The livelihood of the whole town depends on that river! The water level should have been higher! I figured the most likely cause was something blocking the cave with the underground spring that feeds the river. Maybe a beaver dam! So I decided to poke around. I raced down to the riverbed and started walking upriver to search for the problem.

If I had thought it through, I would have met you and given you the raft. I would have brought the issue up with the city council and gotten a crew together to investigate. But I wasn't thinking clearly.

It was almost dark by the time I arrived at the cave. There were no beaver dams or boulders blocking the river.

I decided I *would* talk to the council in the morning. For now, I just had to go back and find you. I looked around and noticed a stream of smoke coming from the top of the cliff. *Perfect!* I thought. *That's coming from Fergus's house. I'll find out if he's seen anything and ask him for a ride back to my car.*

It didn't take long to reach the top of the cliff—it was really more of a steep hill. I lifted my cowboy hat to wipe the sweat off my brow and dropped it in shock. I had expected to see the smoke rising from Fergus's farmhouse, but it was actually coming from a mechanical pump a short distance away. As I walked over to it, Fergus called, "Hey! What are you doing on my land?" He stepped out from behind a silo next to the pump. He didn't realize it was me at first.

"Fergus, it's me, Andrew. So, this is your little hobby farm?" I said.

> (Journal, just for the record, my uncle Fergus has always worked on the family farm Dad inherited. Then, seven years ago, he bought some of his own land, bragging that it was the oldest land in town. But years of farming had drained the soil of its nutrients, and it was unfarmable. Dad had warned Fergus about it, but he didn't listen. He kept trying.)

"Oh. It's you. Aren't you supposed to be at home, having a nice, cozy dinner with your little family?" he asked.

"Yes, but I was just noticing the unusually low river levels for this time of year, and I started to investigate," I told him.

"Always solving everyone's problems, eh?" Fergus said. "Well, was your investigation helpful? Have you saved the town? Or is this just an excuse to trespass on my land—the land that you didn't consider worth a visit until now."

While it may seem odd to you, Hannah, that Fergus was being so hostile, this wasn't our first fight. I knew from the past that the best thing to do was ignore his jibes and focus on what was important. "It's not that I hadn't considered it worthy of a visit. I've just been busy. You've done a surprisingly good job with it," I said. It was true—the land surrounding the pump was bright green with lush grasses, and I could see a field of barley sprouting a few yards away. "Impressive, since I didn't think anything could grow here." I thought my investigation had hit a bit of a dead end—until I noticed this big pump. I couldn't believe what I was seeing. "What are you doing with that?" I pointed to the pump.

Fergus crossed his arms. He looked angry, but he didn't answer, so I walked over to it. **TREASURE HUNTERS LIMITED EDITION WATER PUMP** was etched on the side of the machine.

"Treasure hunters? Water pump? Fergus, what on earth have you been up to?"

"Come on, surely *you* can figure it out. After all, you've always been the talented, smarter older brother." He stood behind me now, and I turned to face him. He was much closer than I had expected, and I backed away from him.

"Fergus, I know we have had our differences in the past. I know you were upset that Mom left the entire farm to me, but in this family, that's how these things have always been done. The oldest inherits the land. I don't see myself as being any better than you. Now, if you really want me to guess, I'd say it looks like you're using this pump to drain the aquifer that supplies the river. Maybe you're using that extra water to support your crops. But that isn't a sustainable solution. Sooner or later, the water will run out, your farm will die, and so will everyone else's," I explained.

"I guess you're not really the smart one, then. You're completely on the wrong track. Sure, the extra water has helped my crops. And I have to admit, I like knowing that my harvest will show the town that I'm a better farmer than you. But I'm not interested in the water. I'm interested in what's under it. That's what's going to save the town. What? You don't think that you—the *glorious Canola King*—are the town's only hero, do you?" He was shouting now. I started to ask if he was kidding, but he cut me off.

"Remember the legend of Wallace "Big Gun" Morrow? Before he disappeared, he hid his treasure. For hundreds of years, people have searched for it in every corner of this town. Well, almost every corner. But there's one place no one has ever looked—in the cave with the spring that feeds the river. An underwater cave is the perfect place to hide a treasure—who would think of checking there? Once I realized this, it didn't take me long to convince Mr. Jenkins to sell me his land—it was, after all, unfarmable. Then all I had to do was start pumping and draining."

He said that last part more calmly, and he took a few steps toward me, forcing me closer to the machine. I stood so close to it now, I could feel its thrumming under my skin. I noticed a huge hole in the ground near the pump's central arm. "How is draining the river going to save the town? Even if you find this treasure, there won't be any water for farming—"

He cut me off again. "You're so attached to this 'farming' idea. There are other industries, you know. The treasure would prove the legend of Wallace Morrow. I'd give some of it to the town and make it rich. Of course, there'd be a very hefty finder's fee for me. And we'd be a tourist capital—a real Wild West town. Heck, we could build a Wallace Morrow theme park if we wanted to!"

A faraway look came over Fergus—and suddenly he

seemed like a stranger. Like some Wild West prospector. Or a character from a cartoon.

"Fergus, you're nuts. As your brother, I'm asking you to stop. There is no treasure!" I said.

Fergus launched himself at me as quick as a bolt of lightning. He caught me off guard. He grabbed me by my collar and pulled me to the edge of the hole, pointing the beam of his flashlight into the water. "Yes! There is!" he said.

I knew that Fergus was not going to listen to reason. He had a real crazed look in his eye. I had to get out of there, so I told him he was probably right and we had to tell the town about it. So they could start planning for it. At this point, I would have said anything to get away from him.

"So that you can take all the credit? So that the Canola King can save the day once again? No—don't patronize me. You got the farm for yourself. You didn't share it with me. Now, it's my turn to have something. And I'm not going to share it with you!" he exploded.

I could tell Fergus didn't plan to share his fantasy treasure with anyone.

He let go of my collar. I don't know if he realized how soft the ground was. I don't know if he saw I was off balance. But the moment he released me, the ground gave out, and I fell into the deep, black hole.

The last thing I saw was Fergus gazing down at me. He was not reaching out to catch me. There was no fear on his face, no sadness, just curiosity. And greed.

My own brother let me drown.

(The ghost went silent. I thought he had finished speaking, but after a second or two, he went on.)

Dad: After I died, I haunted Fergus. I used my energy to haunt him day and night. That's why I didn't come to see you and your mother. I had to get him to confess before I disappeared. I had to get him to tell everyone what had happened. In movies, ghosts can break things, throw things, make a big fuss. But real ghosts, well, I was lucky if I could move his curtains. But no matter how often I called out to him—no matter how many nights I visited him—Fergus insisted there was no ghost. He thought he was imagining me. He thought he was losing his mind.

I didn't want to get you involved in this, but I have no choice. Hannah, you have to tell your mother what happened. She can't let him take over my business. He'll steal everything from the two of you. And tell Rick about the pump. And, whatever you do, stay away from Fergus!

Me: I . . . I need evidence. For them to believe me. Where . . . where is your body?

(Grisly, I know, but that's what they look for in the movies.)

Dad: I don't know. Fergus must have moved it—to cover up what happened. But find the pump. Once you find it, they'll have to believe you.

[COCKADOODLE DOO!]

(Journal, everyone in town knows that annoying sound. It's Uncle Fergus's car horn.

The noise made me jump.

I glanced out the window and saw his bright red sports car pulling up to the mill. As he pounded on the horn, the grain mill door suddenly flew open, and there stood my mom. Sunlight filled the room. When I turned back, the ghost was gone.)

16
CAUGHT IN THE MILL

Mom: She's here!

[Sound of car door opening and slamming shut.]

Fergus: Hannah, what on earth are you doing, hiding in here? You know, it's probably filled with mold. At my age, mold could pose a serious—and I mean serious—threat to my health. Let alone your mother's! And you made her come in here after you!

[Ach, ach, achoo!]

> (That sound is where Uncle Fergus goes into a fit of fake sneezing. Journal, before, the sneezing fit would have been funny. But after hearing about what he did to Dad, I realized that Fergus's act is a tactic to get Mom on his side. To turn her against me.)

F: Back when we used to have a ranch, if a cow ran off, my dad would say, "Welp, we raised and fed and loved that cow—we put a roof over its head—and it lacked sense enough and ran away. You don't chase after flighty cows." I was tempted to tell your mother that, but instead I've been playing nice and searching for you all afternoon! You know, this is exactly why we put chips in our dogs now. You don't want us to put a chip in you, do you? Of course you don't!

> (Journal, for the record, I'm copying this from Dad's tape recorder. I had shoved it into my backpack, and it was still on.)

F: Can you imagine how upset your mother was when she got a call asking why you weren't at school? She was so worried—and it reflects terribly on her as a mother. It looks like she has no control over you. And we both had to rush off and leave all our farm chores right in the middle of the workday. What do you have to say for yourself?

> (I opened my mouth, but Fergus didn't give me a chance to speak.)

F: Oh, I don't need to hear your excuses. Come on.

> (He went to grab my arm, but I dodged him. That weird sound you hear is him chuckling.)

F: You know the runaway cows used to do that, too. Don't make me lasso you.

M: Fergus, that's enough. Hannah, I'm so glad that you're okay. We are going to have a private talk when we get home.

[She gave Fergus a stern glance here.]

M: But, for now, I am happy that you're in one piece. Fergus, I think Hannah and I will walk home. Thank you for your help. We will discuss the business contract tomorrow.

> (Here, while Mom was talking to Fergus, I slipped my hand into my backpack and turned off the recorder.)
>
> ••End of recording••

Fergus gave me one final look—a look that said, "If it were up to me, there really *would* be a chip in you."

As we walked, I wanted to tell Mom not to trust Fergus. I wanted to tell her about the ghost and his story, and that we had to be careful until I figured out if the ghost was telling the truth or not. But I knew she'd never believe anything about a ghost. (Journal, just to be clear: I did think the ghost was my dad, but I didn't know if becoming a ghost had mixed up his memories. Or if a ghost is as honest as the person they used to be. And to get anyone to believe me, I needed to find the proof.)

When I got home, I sat at the kitchen table and watched as my mom whirled into action, cooking dinner with the same dexterity as an experienced fencer. Parry—sauté—strike—chop—defend—steam. Dinner was on the table in twenty minutes flat—not an unusual speed for Mom. We didn't speak as we ate, tension building between us. Mom always made us eat before important conversations because she says you don't think straight when your belly is empty. I was tempted to eat slowly to put off having our "private conversation," but I knew she would notice if I was picking at my food, and it might even offend her if she thought I didn't enjoy my meal. (I always do—Mom is a great cook.) The instant I lifted the last piece of broccoli to my mouth, she whisked the plate away, neatly placed it in the dishwasher, and returned to her seat. The empty table between us felt like an unmarked battlefield.

"Hannah, we need to talk about your recent behavior," she said. "Your uncle was being a bit over the top, but he was correct in saying I was very worried when Ms. Luna called and said you had failed to return to class. I know that Riverway is a safe town. But something did happen to your father here, and we don't know exactly what, so we can't be too careful. It's important for you to let me know where you're going—not only for your own safety but also for my sanity."

I wanted to jump up from my chair and shout, "I think I DO know what happened to him!" But I pressed myself into my seat. I had to be patient. And that, Journal, is not something I'm especially good at. Instead, I forced these words out of my mouth: "I know. I'm sorry. It was a onetime thing, and it won't happen again."

"Hannah, it wasn't just a onetime thing. Last week you missed your assignment due date, then you were late to school, and now you're cutting class? This isn't like you at all."

My heart suddenly started to pound. In some ways, she was right. I had never missed due dates or cut class before. That behavior was "unlike me." But another part of me wanted to tell her that it *was* like me and she didn't have a clue why. Maybe I was just showing who I had really been all along, not some perfect try-hard but somebody who had a problem. If *she* had to sit through a thousand review lessons as electric lights buzzed into her skull and her legs cramped from wanting to jump up and escape; if *she* had to do endless assignments that felt like they'd been completed before they were started; and, on top of that, if *she* had to keep it a secret so nobody noticed her struggle, well then, she would probably act the same way.

But wait. How did she know I missed the assignment due date and was late to school? Ms. Grant said she wouldn't tell anyone—that it was just between us. Had she betrayed me? And, if so, why didn't she tell Mom about *why* I was doing these things? Ms. Grant knew about my investigation.

I considered asking Mom about Ms. Grant, but surely Mom would have brought up my searching for clues if

Ms. Grant had filled her in about everything. Besides, I wanted to make sure it was Ms. Grant before I accused her of anything. But who else could it be? I made a mental note to add Ms. Grant to my investigations: She might be even less trustworthy than I thought.

"Hannah? What do you have to say for yourself?"

I realized that I had zoned out. "I'm sorry, Mom. I've just been having a hard time focusing recently." (That was a colossal understatement.) I almost started to tell her more—about the lights and the legs and the need to run—but something stopped me. Maybe it was the realization that, once it was said, I could never take it back. Her view of me would change forever. Maybe it was the fact that Mom would want to know when it started to get bad, and I'd have to tell her that it had been getting worse since Dad had been gone, and then she might feel guilty. Worse yet, she might start paying even more attention to me, and that would hinder my investigation. Instead, I said, "It won't happen again."

"Well, if you need any help or want to talk about anything, I'm always here." Mom stood and grabbed some papers from the counter, wiping off a few crumbs that had landed on them during her cooking battle. She sat down with a sigh. Her eyebrows scrunched together slightly as she read through them. Clearly, to her, the conversation was over.

Which meant I had to go write my book report, but what can I say? I was curious. "What are those?" I asked.

"Just some business papers for the farm," Mom replied, flipping to the next page.

"What are they for?"

Mom peeked at me over the top of the papers. Something told me she didn't appreciate my questions. "It's just a contract. It'll make it easier for Fergus to help me."

The ghost's—Dad's—warning about Fergus stealing the business rang in my ears. She couldn't sign those papers. "Why do we need Fergus? Can't we just . . . run things ourselves? You know I'll be able to work summers. Plus, I could probably start helping you now. I'm pretty good in math—"

"Hannah, you don't have to worry about these things. Besides, don't you have an assignment to work on?"

The book report. Right. Even with the extended deadline, it was due tomorrow. Plus, I had to call Sam and update him about the ghost. But I needed to make sure that Mom didn't sign those papers. For a moment, my mind was flooded with tasks, and I could feel myself getting overwhelmed. I wanted to call Sam first, but I knew I couldn't miss the deadline again. So I decided to quickly write up the book report and then loop him in. Maybe he'd have some ideas about the contract, too.

"You're right. Thanks for the reminder, Mom. I'm going

to go upstairs and work on my book report."

"Sounds good! I'll bring up some cookies in an hour or two. I love you." The "I love you" was clearly an attempt to decrease the tension caused by our "conversation."

"Love you, too!" I replied as I trotted upstairs.

Now, I'm in my room, and I am supposed to be writing my book report, but I can't think of the first sentence, and without the first sentence, I have no idea what the second or the third or the fourth sentence should be. When it comes to schoolwork, sometimes it feels like my brain stops working. I go from being able to think a thousand things—so many things that I want my brain to just shut up—to not being able to think anything. My brain goes into manual mode. Instead of making a picture out of a room, or reading words, my brain just labels things:

> desk, chair, word, sentence, word, comma, letter, space

To make anything from those parts . . . it takes a lot of work. I can sit and pound on my brain all that I like, but it's not going to do anything automatically. I need to tell it what to think. But when I get like this, all I want to tell my brain is that it's stupid for not working right. So, no matter how much I want to work or think, I'm just not a qualified enough mechanic to get my brain thinking again.

Worse yet, time just keeps ticking away. *Tick tick tick tick tick.* And I want to work. But it's so hard to work. And I want to listen to music. But music doesn't sound the same because I have to tell my brain to listen to all of the music (not just the words or the drums). And I try to just sit with my emotions, but then I get weirdly shifted out of my emotions. Instead of feeling upset, my brain thinks *sadness, anger, tears.* It *thinks* them, it doesn't *feel* them. It feels like I have to breathe manually, to blink manually. And anybody who saw me right now would just see me staring into space. They'd think I was throwing a temper tantrum, or being grumpy, or being lazy. They wouldn't get why I can't move or speak or write.

Nobody can help me when I'm like this. Eventually, I have to speak out loud and say, "Hey, Hannah. What's going on?" That's the only way out. Because only I can say what I need to hear right now. That's why I just started writing words. And now I've written this journal entry. It's hard to write one word at a time, with long pauses in between, but I'll get through this. In fact, I think I just thought of my first sentence for my homework! I'll talk to you later, dear Journal. I'm off to try to write a book report.

Then I'll call Sam. I have to tell him about the ghost.

17
THE WITCHING HOUR HEIST

Journal, I am writing this in total darkness. Well, not total darkness. There's a bit of moonlight sneaking in under the blinds. But it's not enough to see clearly. So, hopefully, this isn't a mess and I'll be able to read it in the morning.

The grandfather clock in the hall just chimed midnight—the Witching Hour. When I was a kid, Dad told me that midnight was called the Witching Hour because that's when magic was at its strongest. He said witches stayed up late so they could cast their spells then.

If I woke up at night to use the bathroom, I'd always check the clock first. If it was anywhere near midnight, I'd hide under my covers. That way, all those witches wouldn't find me. Even though I haven't thought about witches in years, after my encounter with the ghost, I admit I'm feeling nervous being up this late. After all, if ghosts are real, then witches could be, too.

But that's beside the point. You're probably wondering why I'm up so late. Don't worry, I'm not still working on the book report. I finished that *ages* ago, around eight thirty. Then I called Sam to update him on the investigation. We didn't have much time to talk. Sam's mom was making him go to bed at nine because he's "still recovering and needs his rest." I had to give him a quick summary of events: my encounters with the ghost, the story about Fergus, and the possibility that Ms. Grant was not as "confidential" as she claimed to be. He was so excited by what I had to tell him—especially that I finally believed him about the ghost—but he was a little jealous that I could hear the ghost and he couldn't. He wasn't surprised at all about Ms. Grant. "She always seemed snaky," he said. But since tomorrow is Friday, he suggested that we save the Ms. Grant problem for next week. The most important thing was to make sure my mom didn't sign that contract—so we decided that after she went to sleep, I'd creep downstairs and hide it.

Waiting for my mom to go to bed took forever. At first, I tried to read to keep my mind busy. But I felt too on edge to concentrate. All I could manage to do was sit and listen for her to go upstairs. She kept pacing the house, and I swear she unlocked and locked the front door at least ten times before she finally headed up to her bedroom. She never used to do that—she usually went to bed early. But I didn't have time to think about her odd behavior. I waited until there were no sounds from her room. Then I crept downstairs to the kitchen.

Every step felt far too loud—I should ask Tim for some anti-clomping tips. When I got to the bottom of the stairs, I tripped on something and almost shouted, giving away the mission. I caught myself and held my breath, waiting to see if the noise woke her.

Only silence.

Good.

The big kitchen window over the sink let in a lot of moonlight, so it was easy to see everything. Dishes were drying next to the sink. The kitchen chairs had been pushed in, and new place mats had been laid out for breakfast. The counters had been swept clean. And there were no papers in sight.

I backed out of the kitchen, determined not to be upset by this minor hiccup. *If I were an important paper, where would I be?* I thought. Then I remembered Mom brushing the crumbs off the contract. *She probably put it in a place where it wouldn't get dirty. Like my dad's office.*

I turned down the hallway and headed there. The closed office door brought on a terrible feeling of despair. When my dad was here, his door was always open, and he let me wander in any time I liked. The thing is, his office is also really boring. There's nothing besides his desk, some bookshelves, and a big chair with flaking leather. So I hardly ever went in.

And now I regret that. I wish I'd gone in more often. Just to be in there with him.

I'll never have a chance to share that kind of time with him again.

Since he went missing (I still can't say died, not right now), nobody has really been in his office. Some police officers checked it out the day after he disappeared, and I went in to get his tape recorder, but that's about it.

I stepped into the office, and my eyes welled up. I was hit by stale air tinged with a hint of bug spray and dirt—my dad always smelled like bug spray and dirt. It made me miss him more.

It was clear that my mom had been in here. His desk—which was usually kept so neat—was covered in a mess of papers. The pens were no longer in the pencil holder but strewn everywhere.

I expected to have to sort through all kinds of papers to find the contract, but luckily, it was placed neatly on top. I started to read the first page:

> **TRANSFER OF PARTNERSHIP.**

I skimmed the document. It said that Fergus would get fifty percent ownership of the farm. I think that meant we would still get some money from it—but I don't trust Fergus to follow a contract. I picked it up to read it more closely—and a note fluttered to my feet.

Journal, this note was more interesting than anything in the contract. It was from Fergus, written in his squiggly handwriting, and it read:

> Please sign ASAP. Once I'm in charge, you'll have one less thing to think about. Also, please drop off checkbook at my office tomorrow so we aren't slowed down by this legal process and I can start helping out.
> XX
> Fergus

I rolled my eyes when I read that last sentence. Clearly, Fergus wanted the checkbook so he could begin robbing us, just like my dad warned me. But that's not what really made the note stand out. It was the slight glimmer of gold at the top. A glimmer made from an embossed canola plant. The note was written on my father's stationery. The same stationery I saw in Ms. Grant's office.

I slid the contract between some papers on my dad's

bookshelf. But I slipped the note into my pocket. Mom wouldn't notice it was missing.

Right now, I'm holding it in my hand, watching as the golden canola plant reflects the moonlight. Why does Ms. Grant have a note written on the same paper? What is going on here?

18
OUR FIRST CLUE

Dear Journal,

After class, I handed in the book report to Ms. Luna, who accepted it with a big smile and told me she was looking forward to reading my work—a comment that made me feel guilty. The book report was done but nowhere near perfect.

Sam was waiting for me at my locker. We had fifteen minutes before my appointment with Ms. Grant, so I quickly showed him my notes from the ghost meeting.

"Wow," he said. "This is intense. Are you okay?"

I nodded and grabbed the journal from him. I didn't want him to know I wasn't really okay. And I didn't want him to read all that embarrassing stuff about how hard it was to write my book report. That would make our friendship weird. At least, I thought it would.

"So does this end the mission?" he asked. "I mean, the ghost really seems like your dad."

"The mystery is definitely not solved yet. We have to prove that the ghost is telling the truth. Even if he is my dad's ghost, who knows—maybe ghosts lie? And once we have proof, we'll know for sure that he's my dad and not the Old Mill Ghost trying to trick us."

"But he knew so much about you . . . and Fergus . . ." Sam shrugged.

Journal, I know you know this, but hope is a strange thing. Sometimes it makes you wish for the impossible. Like that Dad wasn't gone. I am not giving up until I have proof—real proof, not some story from a ghost.

"We need to know for sure if the ghost is telling the truth," I said again. "We have to find the pump."

"Okay! We'd better get on it fast—before your mom signs that contract," Sam said. "Meet tomorrow morning?"

"Yes!" I said, and rushed off to face the glitter dragon.

I played along with Ms. Grant's exercises, spoke as little as possible, and learned a new way of humming that was supposed to "align my energies."

Today is Saturday, and I woke up early to gather supplies: three ham sandwiches, a water bottle, two granola bars, my journal, and my flashlight. Sam and I had agreed to meet here, then bike along the Riverway Walk. We were going to try to retrace my dad's steps to see if we could find clues and maybe his footprints, although after four months, I didn't think that would be likely.

Biking instead of walking may not have seemed ideal—it could hinder our ability to notice smaller clues—but since our goal was to reach the end of the river as fast as possible, we had to prioritize speed over precision. Besides, I always enjoyed biking along the slopes of the walk. Dad had taught me how to go down the more challenging rocky parts (the trick is—get this—to stand up on your pedals and keep them flat). It's a bit scary at first, but once you're good at it, you can let go of your brakes and swoop from one hill to the next, barely having to pedal uphill at all.

I went to the garage for my bike and felt a twinge of sadness. My dad's much bigger bike was covered in dust, and the tires were flat. Tears filled my eyes. He always took such pride in caring for his bike.

I walked my bike to the front yard and was greeted by the sight of Sam chatting with Mom. His bike seat was low enough that he could easily keep both feet planted on the ground when he sat on it. Dad would have rolled his eyes—that's poor bike setup. You should at least be standing on your tippy-toes when you're on your seat, or else it's difficult to climb hills. I'd probably told him that a million times, but Sam claimed his way looked cooler than mine. I always said I'd rather look like a dork than have to walk my bike up, which usually ended the argument.

"Hannah! Sam and I were just talking about your bike ride. How fun!" Mom smiled and waved me over. "Do you have enough food for the ride?"

"Yes, Mom. I packed plenty of snacks."

"Perfect! And I see you've got your helmet on. Sam, where is yours?" I looked over at Sam with a mischievous smile. Sam insisted that wearing a helmet was also uncool. At one point, I tried to get away without wearing one—at least when biking around town—but Dad shut down that idea by telling me that brain injuries were uncool.

"Um, I—I didn't bring one. I must have forgotten it at home," he stammered.

"No worries! I'm sure we have an old one of Hannah's somewhere. It might be a bit small, but it'll be better than nothing!" Mom rushed away to the garage. She came back with a bright pink helmet covered in blue flames. She plopped it on Sam's head, denting his gelled hair, and buckled it beneath his chin. "Excellent! Now, you two, stay safe, no off-roading!" she said, and waved as we turned on to the gravel path at the end of our crescent—a shortcut to the nature walk.

Once we were out of hearing range, I snorted with laughter. "That helmet looks very cool."

"Don't you think?" Sam pushed the helmet down farther on his head. "The flames make you go faster." We both giggled and turned left, passing a sign that read:

RIVERWAY WALK
SOUTH ENTRANCE

You might imagine that the Riverway Walk would be peaceful early on a Saturday morning—after all, wouldn't everyone be sleeping in and enjoying their day off? Sam and I had figured as much, especially since everyone was still getting used to being back in school. We were very wrong. It felt as though the entire town had decided to take an early morning stroll. Even if Dad's footprints had survived until now, there was no way they'd remain in this kind of traffic.

Sam rode behind me, and I rang my bell constantly as we weaved through the crowd, our bikes leaving piles of gravel and clouds of dust in our wake.

As we rode along the path, the groups of hikers finally thinned out, allowing Sam to bike beside me. Other than wet leaves making the path slippery here and there, the riding conditions were great for this time of year. As we swooped up and down the pathway, I felt free. The mission seemed like a distant memory, with my attention focused on the fall wind rushing at my ears and the steep climb burning my leg muscles.

About half an hour into our route, we faced a fork in the road. The well-groomed Riverway Walk turned back toward the town, while another trail continued along the river. It was very narrow, and the tall, yellowing grass along the sides covered much of it from view. Up here, thick trees grew beyond the grass, closing off any sight of the town.

"One second," Sam panted, riding behind me. "Let's stop." Even though he was in shape from sports, he wasn't used to these difficult hills. "I'm just going to raise my seat."

I smiled. "Okay," I said. "And we'll take a snack break."

Journal, riding uphill can make you very hungry. We ate every last crumb of the ham sandwiches and granola bars, then continued on. As we climbed higher, the tree line became less dense, and we could tell how far up we'd come. We were at least ten feet above the riverbed. It was easy to see how old cowboys walking these uneven paths could have fallen into a rushing river—which might have been fun, like jumping off a high dive! But the odds of our falling in and taking a swim were exactly none. Instead, we risked tumbling into some puddles.

Finally, the path started to flatten. Up ahead, I spotted a cliff face where the riverbank narrowed. "That must be where the river starts! The place the ghost told me about! That's where the pump should be!"

We biked on. The cliff hadn't seemed that far off, but distances are deceiving in the prairie. All the flat grass makes things seem closer than they are. It took another ten minutes before we reached the cliff.

We stashed our bikes in a sparse grove of aspen trees and walked toward Fergus's property. Moments after we stepped off the trail, our path was blocked by a barbed wire fence that marked the edge of his land.

The ghost hadn't mentioned anything about a fence.

Maybe this wasn't the exact place where Dad had stopped.

Or maybe everything the ghost said was a lie, I thought.

But wait . . . I could see a structure about a hundred yards away.

I hesitated to get too close to the barbed wire fence. You do *not* want to get stuck on one of those fences. They are designed to catch cows. Even a minor scrape could get infected or, worse, give you tetanus. Luckily, not ten feet away, the wire sagged close to the ground, and we could safely climb over it.

Finally, we were near enough to see the structure clearly. Not a pump. It was just a silo. We have a few of them on our farm where we store canola seeds or wood chips. This one looked different from ours. I wasn't sure what it was being used for.

"I don't understand," I said. "I thought this was where the ghost said the pump would be." (To tell you the truth,

Journal, at this point, I didn't know if I was upset or relieved. Because if there was no pump, my dad might really be alive and the ghost I'd spoken to was the Old Mill Ghost.)

We walked closer and saw a sign on the silo with a large skull and crossbones. It said:

WARNING!
POISONOUS PESTICIDE

We stopped right there. Most likely, the entire area had been sprayed with the stuff.

"Maybe the ghost didn't remember the spot exactly right," Sam said. "Maybe this isn't the exact place your father left the path."

"Or maybe the ghost isn't my father and he's playing some kind of trick on us," I said, "because you have to consider everything when you're dealing with a ghost or investigating a suspicious disappearance."

"Either way," Sam said, "this looks like a dead end."

"And we'd better leave," I added. "I don't think Fergus would be happy to see us here."

Sam wandered off ahead of me. As I followed him, my mind started spinning with all the possibilities:

Maybe the ghost was lying.
Maybe this wasn't the right spot.

Maybe Fergus had moved the pump.
Or maybe he had gotten rid of it altogether.

I was so lost in thought, I tripped over a rock and fell.

"Are you okay?" Sam ran over to where I was sprawled on the ground.

"Hey! What's that?" From my seat in the dirt, I spotted a flash of brown in the tall weeds a few feet away. "Let's check it out," I said.

We headed to the dried grass and parted it.

And there, tangled in the weeds, was my dad's cowboy hat. It was half-buried in dried clay. I remembered the odd mid-May combination of rain and frost we had this year. The hat had probably been frozen in the mud, which is why it hadn't blown away.

Tears filled my eyes, and I could barely breathe.

I tenderly dusted the brim off and checked inside to see a golden canola plant engraved in the brown leather trim. This was definitely his hat.

"We'd better get out of here," Sam said. He grabbed my wrist and pulled me toward the trees where our bikes were hidden. "If Fergus catches us with that . . ." I nodded and hurried along with him, gripping the hat tightly.

The ghost said his hat fell off when he saw the pump. So this was definitely the right spot. The hat proved the ghost was my dad and he had been on Fergus's farm before he went missing.

My heart felt like it was breaking all over again.

Once we reached our bikes, I balanced the hat on one end of my handlebars, and we pedaled as fast as we could.

"Are you going to bring the hat to Rick and tell him everything now?" Sam asked.

"Not yet," I said. "Fergus could claim that Dad's hat just blew away. That it had nothing to do with him. We have to find the pump."

19
PLAN A

"See, there are portable pumps like this that are easy to move!" Sam pointed to an image of a machine with two arms, an engine, and two large wheels.

The librarian shushed us.

It was recess on Monday, but instead of heading outside, we had decided to do some quick research to figure out our next steps.

"That's cool," I whispered. "The silo could have been storing water. And if the pump is like that one, Fergus can move it whenever he wants."

"Exactly!" Sam said. "What have you been looking up?"

"Information about rivers. There are lots of different types. Some are fed by glaciers. Others by big lakes. Ours is fed by groundwater in a big underwater cave called an aquifer. The ghost mentioned an aquifer. Usually, the aquifer is refilled by melting snow or rainwater, so the river level stays the same. But if something drains the aquifer too fast, then the water level will go down and the river will dry up. Some people blame canola farming for draining the spring too fast, but we've been farming for decades and the water level only seriously started to go down in the past five years. And Fergus bought his farm seven years ago."

"Whoa." Sam shook his head.

"We need to snoop around Fergus's farm. I bet he's hiding the pump there," I said. I pictured Fergus's property. He had a lot of land that we'd have to search. "I think we're going to need help. Let's ask Tim. He's an experienced snoop, and he's light on his feet."

Sam made a face, which surprised me because he's usually very friendly.

"What's wrong?" I whispered.

"I'm worried about anyone else knowing what we're up to. This has to be kept a secret. We don't want Fergus finding out."

Sam was right. But Tim had been reliable so far, and we really needed the help.

"How about we tell him only part of the story? We won't mention my dad or the ghost. We'll just tell him we think Fergus has an illegal pump. Tim is very serious about people breaking the rules. I know he'll want to keep that secret to catch the culprit."

Sam agreed and ran off to get in some soccer before the bell rang. I went looking for Tim. I found him guarding the playground door. "Hey, Tim! We need your help again!"

"More information on Ms. Grant? I heard that you met with her." His eyes glinted with curiosity. For a moment, I was hit by a wave of shame—but I brushed past it. I needed to focus on the Fergus problem.

"No, but I do have some updates there." Tim's question reminded me about my father's stationery. I wondered if he knew any clues about how it had landed on Ms. Grant's desk. Sometimes he delivers the mail for the principal. But I needed to take things one step at a time: We had to deal with Fergus first.

"I'll fill you in about that later," I said. "But right now, I need to talk to you about some spy work. Have you ever done any?"

Tim's chest puffed up with pride. "Spy work? Like what?"

"Like . . . snooping." I lowered my voice so some nearby kids wouldn't hear.

"I may have some experience with that." Tim inspected his fingernails. "What do you have in mind?"

I leaned close to his ear and told him about the search for the pump. "So, can we count you in?"

The second bell rang. "Absolutely." Tim smiled. "Now, off to class before I give you a late slip." He waved me off abruptly, and I disappeared through the door and into the hall, my mind already swimming with plans for the mission.

We needed to:

1. Find a time when we could all go.
2. Find a time when we could all go and no one would be looking for us.
3. Find a time that Fergus wouldn't be around.

Journal, for a week, it seemed like the search would never happen. Sam was busy with soccer, softball, *and* baseball practice, and Tim had taken on extra hall monitor shifts at the preschool.

For my part, my distraction in school was starting to catch up with me. Because I'd missed some class time and hadn't absorbed much in the classes that I did attend, I had to *study* for the first time in my life. Let me tell you, Journal, studying is basically one long, endless review class. But until we knew what Ms. Grant was up to, I needed to stay under her radar, so I couldn't let my grades slip or miss another deadline.

I could feel the case going cold, and waiting to visit Fergus's farm was almost unbearable. But then an opportunity suddenly presented itself the following week during Mr. Lewis's science class.

"Hello, everyone! I hope you've had a restful weekend and enjoyed the Fall Harvest Festival," Mr. Lewis said.

Some students nodded and started talking about the hundred-pound pumpkin Ms. Bailey grew. I, for one, had been unable to go to the town's annual celebration due to a hefty math assignment that I'd put off till the last minute. Mom had tried to convince me to go to the festival with her, to take a break from my hard work, but I finally felt motivated, and I didn't want to lose steam.

Besides, Dad's canola always won the "Cream of the Crop" competition. Going there with him to stand on the podium when he collected his prize—a porcelain pig holding corn on the cob, courtesy of Joe's Antique Emporium—had been our thing. No matter how cheery the lights or sweet the cotton candy, attending the festival without him would just hurt too much.

"Well, for those of you who had a chance to attend, this announcement won't be much of a surprise. As you all know, every year the grade six class visits the winning 'Cream of the Crop' farm to learn more about agriculture and ecology."

Usually, the class visited the Canola King's Kingdom. My dad's farm. Even before he officially knew he'd won, Dad would set up the tour weeks in advance, working extra hours to clean the barns and store dangerous equipment. But for the first time in twenty years, there was a new winner.

"This year, we'll be visiting Mr. Fergus Edwards's barley crop!" Mr. Lewis paused as though he expected a gasp of shock or a round of applause. Instead, he received a half-hearted yawn and the sound of somebody's chair squeaking.

I wasn't shocked either. The ghost said Fergus's barley was growing surprisingly well. He said Fergus was using water stolen from the rest of us to grow it. It all fit.

Misinterpreting the class's boredom for disappointment, Mr. Lewis continued. "Trust me, everyone. This is exciting! Part of what makes this trip so unique is the mystery behind it. Most of us thought that Fergus's farm was unfarmable. That makes Fergus's barley a sort of miracle!"

I rolled my eyes. Fergus's "miracle crop" wasn't a miracle if you knew the real story. I couldn't wait to find the pump—then everyone would know the truth about Fergus.

"He claims that it grew with a secret method handed down to him from the previous owner: the Ye Olde Jenkins Family Method. When we visit, we will learn all about this method! Just think of how helpful it could be to offset the effects of over-farming and drought! Plus, if land remains farmable for a longer period, we won't have to clear as many new plots! Isn't that exciting!" Mr. Lewis was going off on one of his rants—a highlight of his class. Somebody in the back of the class whooped, and Mr. Lewis finally received the encouragement that he craved.

"I'm sure you'll all nerd out as much as me once we're on the field trip. I've printed some permission slips. Please get them signed by your parents or guardians and return them by Thursday. The field trip will take place next Monday, so it's extra important that nobody hands them in late! Trust me, I'm *not* going to track down anybody who doesn't get their form in on time!" Mr. Lewis tried to give the class a stern, no-nonsense look, but its effect was reduced by his reputation: Everybody knew that Mr. Lewis *always* tracked down anybody who was missing a permission slip. He just couldn't stand the idea of somebody missing out on a "great educational opportunity!"

This was the best news ever! The field trip would finally allow us to snoop around Fergus's farm.

Journal, you'd imagine all this would make me feel one-hundred-percent better. But it hasn't because the trip is still a week away, giving me too much time to think. My mind keeps circling around all the ways Dad could still be alive.

Maybe he's in the big city, trying to convince people to save the river. Maybe he was kidnapped by jealous farmers and forced to grow canola for a different town. Maybe he's in disguise, living under a different name—the Wheat King.

I picture him returning. Apologizing for being gone so long. Telling us how much he missed us and suggesting we all go for a bike ride.

But then I remember the sound of the ghost's voice. And finding the cowboy hat caked with mud. And Fergus's mysterious prize-winning crop. And I want to find the pump. I want everyone to know the truth about my father's disappearance.

But if we find the pump, I'll have to give up those maybes. And I'm not sure I'm ready for that yet.

20
WAITING IS
THE WORST

Journal,

Waiting is the worst. Our whole investigation is stalled until we can get to Fergus's farm next week. The more excited I get about the field trip, the slower time seems to move.

Paying attention in class has been particularly excruciating. For example, did you know—this is going to shock you—that you can use the same greater than or less than symbols to show the difference between percentages and fractions, not just decimals and fractions? A complete twist—I know!

In case you can't tell, I'm being sarcastic. Yet most of math class today was dedicated to this simple topic. At first, I tried to focus, telling myself that "you never know when you might look away from the board and miss something important." But ten minutes into the lesson, it was clear that Ms. Knugen thought this concept was worth an entire hour. As I stared at the whiteboard, my eyes felt like they were melting out of my skull. My legs screamed to me: We are meant to *run*. Why are we *sitting* here? To try to get rid of some of my energy, I clicked my pen.

"So, if 0.11 is bigger than 1/10, then which way should the symbol face?" *Click.* I imagined the sound as my brain taking a picture of the information.

"Mary?" *Click.* "It should face 0.11." *Click.* "Correct." *Click.* "Now, let's try a more complex question." *Click.* "Whoever is clicking your pen, please stop. It is *very* distracting."

My face instantly turned red even though I hadn't been called out by name. I started to write, but that last click had retracted the tip.

Grimacing, I clicked the pen one more time.

Ms. Knugen whipped around from the board, sternly looking for the pen-clicking menace. There was a tense moment of silence; then she tapped her foot twice (a warning) and returned to the board.

Without the pen clicking, my brain fully refused to pay attention to the next problem. I considered tapping my feet, but that was probably going to get me in trouble, too.

My mind kept returning to our upcoming plans. So I decided I would write everything down. Sometimes moving things from my brain to a piece of paper helps me think more clearly. I wrote this list and taped it here:

Evidence
Ghost's story

Dad's hat

Note on Dad's stationery in Dad's office

Things That We Think We Know
Ghost knows enough to be Dad

Fergus is draining river, using water to make prize crop

Fergus is trying to steal our farm

Fergus let Dad drown

Things That Still Don't Make Sense
Pump wasn't where ghost said it would be

Note on Dad's stationery in Ms. Grant's office

Next Steps
Will check Fergus's farm for pump—Monday

Find note in Ms. Grant's office—???

As I wrote the list, I felt a jolt of electricity. For a moment, I could completely focus. The buzzing of the lights went away. The drone of Ms. Knugen's voice faded into the background. My legs stilled. My heartbeat became regular. I was in "the zone," as Dad would say. And once the list was finished, the feeling of electricity stayed with me as I reread the last item:

> Find note in Ms. Grant's office—???

That note could be connected to our mystery, and THAT'S what we should be doing now, I thought. *While we wait for the field trip, we should get that note.*

"Hannah? What do you think?" Ms. Knugen's voice interrupted my trance. My eyes rocketed up from my notebook to the board, which, to my horror, was now covered in symbols that I'd never seen before. Some of the less than symbols were now adorned with small lines like this: $\leq$. Worse yet, the familiar equal sign now wore a squiggly hat ($\cong$). And letters, too, had suddenly appeared. What were letters doing in math class?

I sat paralyzed as the new symbols swam before my eyes. Instinctively, I glanced down at my notes, only to see the list, which now seemed to mock me.

My eyes returned to the board, desperate to see if I could recall *something, anything,* so that Ms. Knugen wouldn't know I hadn't been paying attention.

"Can you please repeat the question?" I asked, trying to stall.

Ms. Knugen exhaled, her breath whistling out of her nose, and I swore I heard somebody in the back of the class giggling. *They are just laughing at her. Not at you*, I thought. But I wasn't convinced.

"If $x=3$ and $y=4$, then which way should the sign point, toward $10\%x$ or $1/2y$?" Ms. Knugen asked.

My breath felt bottled up in my chest.

Come on brain, think.

Just say something, I thought, but I didn't want to risk being wrong.

I glanced to the side and noticed that several students had shifted their bodies to turn around and look at me.

What could I say? "Oh, I wasn't paying attention"? That might work if I was somebody else. Besides, I had already asked her to repeat the question. Honesty now would just reveal my previous lie.

I looked back down at my notes. *If I had paid attention, this wouldn't be happening. Now everyone will know there's something wrong with me.*

"It's okay, this is a tricky question. In the interest of time, I'll give this one away." Ms. Knugen wrote a symbol on the board.

$$10\%x < \tfrac{1}{2}y$$

The squeak of her marker drilled into my head. I wrote the answer in my math notebook, but it didn't make much sense to me. I felt as if an enormous weight was pushing down on my shoulders. I wondered if it could press me so tightly, I'd fold up and fit in a box.

Even though everyone had turned back to face the board, I could still feel their eyes on me. I imagined giant question marks hovering above their heads and imagined them thinking:

"What was that about?"

"Is she always this weird?"

"Did you hear she's been seeing Ms. Grant?"

For the rest of the class, my pen drifted across my page, diligently taking notes. But I didn't understand the topic at all. I'd missed the magic key to comprehending any of it. When the bell rang, I shoved my notebook into my backpack, avoiding eye contact with everyone. I wanted to run out of the classroom as fast as I could and go home. But the entire school day still stretched ahead of me.

As I turned the corner on the way to science class, Sam tapped my shoulder.

"Hey, are you all right? You seem upset," he said.

"No. Not upset. Everything's fine." I might have felt better if I had confided in him, but I couldn't do it. My reputation had been damaged enough for the day.

To make myself feel better, I reached into my backpack for my list and showed it to Sam. "Sam, I know what we have to do next. We have to get the note in Ms. Grant's office. We have to see what it says. It could be important evidence."

"Okay," Sam said. "But *how* are we going to get it?"

"The *how* isn't the problem, Sam," I said. "The problem is the *who*."

21
THE GLORIOUS TALE AND TRAGEDY OF TIM THE HALL MONITOR

Dear Journal,

Today, we learned about epic poems, and I can't get the rhyme scheme out of my head. Apologies in advance—I did the best I could and promise to become a better rhymer when time allows.

> Hear ye, hear ye! Come hear this tale,
> Of a boy's bravery—incomparable in scale.
> We'll start in the middle (that's how the story goes),
> And how the story ends, only Tim knows.

Click! That's the sound Tim's key made as it slid into Ms. Grant's door. Tim (previously known as Tim the Timid) was the Hall Monitor of lore! Legend has it that, even as a three-year-old student, Tim was ever on the lookout for a possible truant. This past, this history, made his break-in more shocking: What could convince this hero to open a door without knocking? Why, Tim is following an important plan: He must save Hannah the Honorable—he's the only one who can.

This all began during a boring lunch hour when I offered our Tim a title of magnificent valor.

"Tim," I quietly said, "we need to find out what Ms. Grant knows, and I have an idea I'd like to propose. If you complete this mission, which is very specific, we will all be calling you Tim the Terrific."

"Why, dear Hannah, I am already terrific!" Tim boasted, discarding the new honorific. "Who else has access to the sacred keys? Who else can be late to any class he may please? Who else has the right to patrol the hallways? Why, I am Tim the Terrific, now and always."

"Dear friend, dear Tim, all this is true. But don't let your power get the best of you. While, to the teachers, you are dependable and tall, the other kids don't trust you at all. Think of a kid running late to class, or somebody who forgot to grab their bathroom hall pass. Imagine their fear when they turn the corner, only to see you, Mr. Law and Order! Why, Tim, they think that you're a boring grown-up. Do you want to change this? Time to own up!"

Tim sat and stared and played with his shoe. He'd never considered this. He didn't have a clue. "Hannah, oh Hannah, tell me what to do! I want to be as well-liked as you."

"What we need is proof that Ms. Grant is a snitch, but her office is locked—that's our hitch. Tim, as the keeper of the keys, you've claimed you can open any door you please. If this is indeed true, then this is a task for no one but you. You must sneak into Ms. Grant's office and look for some proof and also the note on Dad's stationery. It'll show us the truth!" Even though Tim liked a challenging caper, I could see he didn't want to be a rule breaker. He needed encouragement to see his task wasn't wrong. I needed to remind him to please remain strong.

"I'm aware that you took a serious vow—to use your keys for what the law will allow. But I am not asking you to break the rules for no reason: Ms. Grant is committing the worst kind of treason! She's claiming to be a safe, secretive friend, but it's all part of her game of Let's Pretend. So entering her office will be far from criminal, and, if you're careful, the damage will be minimal. So, Tim, what do you say? Will you become a hero today?"

"A hero?" Tim asked. "And you're sure I'll be fine?" I nodded, hoping that he wouldn't decline. "Well," Tim said, "I know my decision: I will accept this perilous mission."

Now we return to the sound of the key, and of Tim's break-in mastery. *Click* was the sound that Tim's key made in the door. *Swish* was the sound as the door brushed the floor. At any moment, Tim expected an alarm to ring out in the hall. But he was greeted by silence, by no noise at all. He peeked inside to check for the slumbering creature, but no such evil was there, no dragon, no teacher.

Even though Ms. Grant was not in the room, there was something about her cushions that spelled certain doom. Maybe if Tim stepped on them, an alarm would sound. Maybe they would burst with acid and melt Tim to the ground. Tim shivered at that last thought. He must not touch the cushions—or he might get caught.

A less brave Hall Monitor might have turned back. Tim almost did, in fact, want to backtrack. But he remembered Hannah's important admission—that he, Tim the Monitor, was the right man for the mission. Tim, although smart and well-connected, had never before been specially selected. Especially not by one of his peers, so he took a deep breath and ignored his fears. Our brave hero did not crack. He stepped into the office, ready to attack.

In legends, in poems, in stories of old, there were tales of princes who courted danger, we're told. These heroes, though grown-ups, though strong and hale, sometimes—accidentally—would try but fail. But Tim, dear Tim, our man of honor, had no fear he'd be a goner. You see, Tim had been trained in an ancient tradition: a game called the Floor Is Lava, for kids with ambition. To make it to the cabinet, he played the game in reverse. That is how Tim reached the cabinet without making things worse.

He grabbed the top drawer and pulled with great might. But the cabinet would not open without a fight. He put his foot up and tugged some more, but nothing, no force, would move that drawer. He then noticed a hole—a hole for a key—and he grinned and broke into a fine dance of glee. This was a job for Tim, the key master: If he had the right key, this task would go faster. He flipped through his ring with amazing speed and looked for the key that he would need. But every key was either too big or too small. I guess Tim didn't have the right key at all.

Some would give up. Some would despair. Some would stamp their feet or pull at their hair. Tim, however, was not the type to explode. He was too wise, too smart, and now very bold. So he swept away any shadow of gloom and carefully looked around the room. If he concentrated hard, Tim the Terrific knew, he would come up with just the right clue.

"Wait! Hannah told me!" he shouted with glee. "The rainbow cushion—that's where I'll find the key!"

Tim found the key. His victory was sweet. In the drawer he found Dad's stationery and a Parents and Guardians Only sheet!

Tim was so excited as he dashed out the door—he forgot all about the key he'd left in the drawer. Oh Tim, why must some good heroes fail? Will there not be a happy ending to your tale?

Tim gave the evidence to joyful me. "Congratulations, Tim," I said with glee. "Your actions today were truly brave! You are a terrific knight, not a lowly knave."

This victory, though great, was very short. The next day, Tim was called to Ms. Grant's court. What happened there, well, I nearly choked. His title as Hall Monitor was revoked.

"Tim, I am very disappointed in you. Now, what do you think I should do? You broke the rules." Ms. Grant sighed. "That, you'll agree, cannot be denied."

"Ms. Grant—"

"No—don't speak! There are no excuses. I know what happened. I know what the truth is. My private cabinet drawer was open, but the door to my room was not broken! You're the only one who holds the keys, but this does not mean you enter here when you please. You are no longer a monitor, and please don't moan. I will not change my mind, no matter how loud you groan. Tim, I now dub thee Crossing Guard. Take this orange vest. And remember in the future: Following rules is for the best!"

Thus ends our tale of the brave hero Tim, who lost his title, but not on a whim. Tim sacrificed his keys for his friend, something that was well worth it in the end. Whenever you help us cross the road to the bus, know that, Tim, you will always be Hall Monitor to us.

22
THE PARENTS AND GUARDIANS ONLY SHEET AND A SUSPICIOUS NOTE

When Tim handed me two sheets of paper during lunch hour today, I was filled with a sense of silent satisfaction. Here, in my hands, was some solid evidence—proof of Ms. Grant's treachery. The first piece of evidence was a Parents and Guardians Only sheet. Unlike the lime-green For Kids sheet, this was white and printed in a standard, boring typeface. As I smoothed out the wrinkles in the paper, I reread it for like the thousandth time.

> **FOR PARENTS AND GUARDIANS**
>
> Don't you want to know what your child is *really* up to?

I believe that the parent-child relationship is the most important gift we will ever receive. Contrary to popular belief, student-teacher confidentiality distances children from their parents and guardians and pushes them toward harmful habits like poor dietary choices, procrastination, and video games. Think of me as your hotline into your kid's brain. I will find out exactly what is going on and keep you updated on your child's health.

My three-step technique is guaranteed to solve any problem your child is having at school *and* at home:

1. Bond with the student: Become friends with your little angel, and they will let me know exactly what's going wrong in their world.

2. Report back to you: I will report your child's activities and supplement this with my expert advice.

3. Monitor the situation: I will continue to bond with your student, monitor the program's success, and keep you informed.

With this technique, you will quickly know exactly what your child has been up to.

"Hotline into your kid's brain," "report back to you," "monitor the situation." Ms. Grant wasn't—isn't—my friend. She is a spy!

And what was on my father's stationery was even worse:

> Ginger,
>
> Barbara just told me about Hannah's late paper. How upsetting! As her uncle, I am very concerned.
>
> When you ask Hannah about the paper, see what you can find out about what she's been up to. She mentioned that she thought she'd do a better job finding her dad than the police. What a burden for a child to carry! Is she really trying to find her dad? Definitely ask her about that. I care about her so much; she shouldn't have such big problems on her mind.
>
> Don't worry about bothering her mother with any of this—she's upset enough. It'll be our little secret. Maybe we can discuss it over the dinner that you suggested. Sometime soon?
>
> XX
> Fergus

When I first read the note, I was flooded with energy. Everything became so clear. Fergus was asking Ms. Grant to spy on me because he was worried about me looking into Dad's disappearance. That was a clear sign of his guilt.

And Ms. Grant was actually helping him! She was helping a potential murderer! I knew it was time to tell my mom the truth.

Fueled—no, blinded—by my newfound certainty, I strutted home, mentally preparing what I'd say. "Mother, I have to tell the tale of a bloody deed."

No, that sounded too much like those old books we were reading in class.

"Rejoice, Mother, for I have solved the mystery." Still the same problem. Plus, I was imagining that line with trumpets, and that would *never* happen.

"Mom, I have something important to tell you. Ms. Grant is a spy. Also, Uncle Fergus murdered Dad." Perfect. Understated. Direct. I would announce it as I walked into the kitchen.

Yet no such fantasy occurred. I entered an empty house. Mom must have been working late. I sat down at the kitchen table, expecting her to arrive any minute.

While I waited, time dragged on. My stomach started growling. I forced myself to sit still. The increasing grumbling of my stomach marked off the hours.

Mom finally pulled into the driveway as the sun went down. She entered the house looking slightly frazzled. I restrained my urge to ambush her with my news, instead making small talk. "How was your day?" I asked.

"Good! Very busy. We are deciding who we'll keep on for maintenance tasks over the winter and who we will have to lay off," she said.

"That doesn't sound like very much fun at all," I said, and Mom nodded.

Even though she hadn't even been inside for five minutes, she was already starting to prepare dinner. Tonight, it was something involving onions, lemons, tomatoes, and chicken. It is one of Dad's favorites. No, it *was* one of Dad's favorites. I have to get used to thinking about Dad in the past tense. Did Mom think about Dad in the past tense now? No longer *liking* things. *Liked* things. I wasn't sure. At that thought, I knew I had to tell her.

"Mom, I have something important to talk about."

She put aside the knife she was using to chop onions and wiped tears from her eyes. "What is it, Hannah?" She sat on the chair facing me.

I paused, trying to decide what I should tell her about first: Ms. Grant or my dad? I figured I'd start off with the easier of the two.

"Okay, this might sound like a bit of a stretch, but just listen, please. At the beginning of the school year, I started to see Ms. Grant. She wanted to talk about 'my loss' and assist me with things and stuff."

Mom nodded as though she already knew this.

"Well, I told her a lot of confidential stuff. And, it turns out, I was wrong to trust her." I grabbed my journal from my backpack and opened it to the page with the Parents and Guardians Only sheet. "We got this from her office. You can read it. Basically, it says that she isn't confidential—that she's a spy for parents who might need her help."

"I think you're taking this a bit too literally, honey. Sometimes parents have to talk to teachers to make sure their kids are okay," Mom said.

"That's not the point!" I snapped. My stomach grumbled in agreement. "The point is she said that everything would be confidential, and she's lying to kids. How can anybody trust her when she's going around blabbing to parents or relatives or, honestly, who knows who? If she's going to tell one person, why not tell the entire school? Why not say, 'Hannah Edwards is seeing me for help! Tune in at four to get my bulletin!'"

"Hannah, I'm sure she isn't *blabbing* about you to just anybody."

"No, she isn't telling *just anybody*. She's just telling the worst possible person: Uncle Fergus!"

"Uncle Fergus?" Mom sounded surprised.

"Yes, and it's even worse than you think because Uncle Fergus is . . . he's a bad guy."

Mom stared at me in that weird, silent way grown-ups do. The way that makes their eyes look all soft and sad but their faces look hard and strong. The look says, "You are a kid, and you don't know everything." I hate that look. She took a deep breath. I hate when adults take deep breaths—it's never a good sign.

"Hannah, Fergus isn't a bad guy. Sometimes he might be a bit over the top, but that doesn't change the fact that he cares about you and wants to make sure you're okay. We both do."

She just didn't get it. "Mom. He IS a bad guy. I wasn't sure about it at first, because I wasn't sure if I could trust the ghost—"

"Ghost? Hannah, what are you talking about?"

"Dad's ghost! Look, let me start at the beginning. That will make the most sense. A few weeks ago, Sam saw a ghost in the Old Grain Mill that looked like Dad, and I didn't believe him, so we had a séance, and we sort of contacted it, but we kept getting interrupted. Then one day I decided to check out the ghost myself—that's why I was late to school—and I met him, and he told me that he was Dad and that Uncle Fergus was draining the river to get to some buried treasure, and then Dad fell into a well, and Uncle Fergus didn't do anything to help him.

Obviously, I didn't believe him right away, so Sam and I biked to Fergus's property, and we found Dad's hat."

The words rushed out of me in one giant breath. I knew that I was talking too fast. That there was probably a better way of telling this, but I wanted her to hear all the details. I wanted her to feel the flow of the story, to have the same sense of anticipation, to understand that I'd really checked each and every fact before making any accusations.

"A ghost? Hannah, there are no such things as ghosts." Mom's voice was flat. Not angry. Not sad. Flat.

"But I have proof. I have Dad's hat. And I'm going to get more proof. I'll get the hat." Before she could protest, I ran up to my room, grabbed the hat, and raced back to the kitchen.

A cloud of dust formed a halo around the hat as I triumphantly slapped it on the table. Mom gingerly picked it up, checking the inside for the engraved canola plant. Then she looked up at me. I expected her face to show grief, but instead, she looked angry.

"How long have you had this?" She continued before I could speak. "The moment you found it, you should have brought it straight to me or Rick. Hiding it was really irresponsible of you." Before, being called irresponsible would have made me crumble. Not anymore.

"I wanted to be sure of the whole story before I did anything."

"What story, Hannah? So you found this on Fergus's farm—are you sure it didn't blow there? Or that Fergus was even aware of it? I'm certain that your uncle would have brought it to the police if he'd known about it."

"But he wouldn't have! That's the whole point! It's evidence of his guilt," I said.

"Yes, according to a story that you heard from a ghost. Hannah, I know how much your father's loss has affected you, and I know you want answers, but creating this unbelievable tale to blame your uncle is taking things a step too far. I won't tell him about this. It will hurt his feelings. But you need to make sure you don't get caught up in stories to avoid feeling your grief. You need to work through it. This is exactly why I asked Ms. Grant to talk to you."

23
THE NEFARIOUS SUNNYSIDE SCHOOL RETREAT

The world reeled. My own mother was my betrayer. I wanted to tell her that she could have just talked to me. That I'm not some angsty kid making up stories to hide from reality. That it would have helped if she had discussed Dad's disappearance with me instead of burying the whole thing. But instead, I barked, "So you have been spying on me?"

"Hannah, I reached out to Ms. Grant because her job is to help kids like you. Kids who might be feeling a bit sad or scared after something big happens. It's not because I don't love you or trust you. I just wanted you to have a place to talk—a place where you could feel safe," she said.

"And then you decided to listen into that space?" I said.

"Hannah, I love you. I think you feel that you have to hold yourself to very high standards, but your father's disappearance is beyond your control, and it's not your responsibility to fix it. There is clearly too much stress here for you. And being here limits your ability to move on because everything is reminding you of our loss. But we have come up with a possible solution."

Journal, this is when Mom grabbed a stack of papers from her briefcase, sifting through them until she found a brochure. The front was covered in some odd fern drawings, and it had been printed to look slightly worn and weathered—almost like papyrus. In overdone swirly type, the title—**SUNNYSIDE SCHOOL RETREAT: THE SCHOOL OF STILLNESS AND SELF-LOVE**—hovered above a blue cross-legged figure.

I pushed the brochure away—I didn't need to read it to know that it would praise the importance of friendship and nature to solve all my problems. Or that some silly saying in its name could possibly be a substitute for my dad.

Mom gently pushed the brochure back toward me. "It's a sort of spa school! There are students who stay there all year round, but we thought you could just try it for two weeks and see how you feel! We think it's the perfect place to recover from the trauma of your dad's disappearance. Look, they even have frogs!"

She opened the brochure and pointed to an image of a single frog sitting on a lily pad in the middle of a tranquil pond. A kid, older than me, maybe fourteen, with sandy blond hair, stared at the frog with a grin on his face. To adults, the kid probably looked joyful. At ease. But I could see that the smile wasn't reaching his eyes, which were screaming, "Help me! They've stitched this smile on to my face, and I can't close my mouth!" I shuddered. "Who is this 'we' that's making all my life decisions for me?" I asked.

Mom furrowed her brow. She clearly thought one image of a frog would have improved my mood. "Myself, Ms. Grant, and your uncle. The spa school was actually Fergus's idea; one of his friends sent their son to this place after there was a combine accident on their farm. Apparently, it was transformative! Ms. Grant has called ahead and checked on the school's credentials, and she completely agrees that it is the right decision."

Fergus *and* Ms. Grant were conspiring against me. He was definitely using her crush on him to manipulate her. I knew Fergus was too slippery to tell her the *real* reason he wanted me to go to the school—to send me out of town so he could finish draining the river. But even though Ms. Grant didn't know she was being used, I was still angry that she would actually help him get rid of me.

I let out a huge sigh. My mother was taking advice from a murderer (who was trying to get me out of the way) and his lovestruck accomplice.

My mom noticed my irritation and placed a hand on my shoulder. "I had to share my concerns with somebody, Hannah, especially now that your father is gone. Fergus was really worried about you when I told him about Ms. Grant's reports. And he's been very helpful. Can you please give this school a chance? For me?" She looked at me earnestly.

People say that eyes are the windows to the soul. If that's the case, Mom's soul said, "I am still sad about your dad, and you have not been making it easier on me. Please give me a break."

I wondered what my eyes were saying. Did they reflect my anger at being spied on? Or maybe they showed guilt: I never wanted to be a problem.

I broke eye contact when I noticed a stack of papers on the corner of the table. They looked just like the contract I had hidden from her. Fergus must have sent her another copy.

"What are those?" I asked, dodging her question. "Do they have more information on the school?"

"No, honey. These are just a formality for the farm."

"A formality?"

"Well, you know it's been hard for me to make all the decisions for the farm since I was never really that involved with it. Unlike your father, I didn't grow up on farms, so it takes me a lot longer to do things. Fergus has offered to ease the load by taking over the business."

"Mom, don't sign those papers."

GRRRRRRRSLOSHGURGLE. My stomach rumbled.

"Well, *that* explains your stress! You know you can't think straight with an empty stomach. Let me finish getting dinner started." It was clear Mom didn't want to talk about this. She whirled up from her chair and returned to chopping onions.

"Mom, I'm not hungry! Why would you give away the farm? What if Dad comes back?" Not that I believed he was coming back. But maybe, I thought, if I said that, it would get her to listen.

"Hannah, it's just a formality. Your uncle will be able to run the business better this way. Besides, look at how successful he has been with his barley crop!"

I clenched my fists. Somehow every adult in town had fallen for Fergus's "miracle" crop. I wanted to tell Mom that Fergus and his crop were frauds. And worse—he was a murderer! But if I told her now, she'd probably discount the pump as another far-fetched tale. Better to wait until after I'd found it. Then she'd have to believe me.

Onions sizzled as she tossed them into the pan, and the kitchen was filled with their savory aroma. I had to concentrate so the smell wouldn't distract me.

"Everything is going to be fine," she went on. "Spa school will be lots of fun—like a vacation! And you'll probably meet such nice kids!" she added as she plopped the chicken into the pan.

"A vacation could be nice." I struggled to lie.

Mom turned around, flashing a smile of victory. "Perfect! I'll call the school and let them know. You'll start one week from Monday."

When I set the table for dinner, I offered to bring the contract to Dad's office. As I did, I swiped one random sheet from the stack. Dad always told me the law works slowly—who knows how long it would take before people realized the page was missing, and how long it would take to replace it? Either way, it should delay Fergus long enough for me to show my mom the truth.

Journal, there is no way that I am going to spa school.

On the field trip on Monday, Sam, Tim, and I will find that pump—and we'll make sure everyone finally knows the truth about Fergus.

24
MY NOTES ON THE
FIELD TRIP
TO FERGUS'S FARM

Dear Journal,

    Apologies for using you for class work, but Mr. Lewis told us to take notes and I forgot my science notebook at home. I'll rewrite them later, so I won't have to tear out any of your precious pages.

    Even though Sam and I had been on Fergus's land when we were searching for the pump, I'd actually never been to his farmhouse—he never invited us—so my visit was just as fresh as anyone else's.

    The first thing I noticed as I stepped off the bus was how little the land resembled a farm. Typically, farms around here are bustling with people and machines. No matter where you stand, somebody will come by and tell you that you need to get out of the way. Even on off days, the dozens of sheds and garages and machines parked across the land will make a farm seem busy. Fergus's farm had none of those things: There were no machines, no sheds, no animals roving across the yard. The only real farm-like structure was the old barn, which I could just make out behind the trees that lined the main yard.

Fergus had torn down the old farmhouse that used to be on the property and built a modern monstrosity made almost entirely of concrete and corrugated steel. The red steel balcony that was clearly repurposed from a shipping container was a sad attempt to capture your attention, saying, "Hey, here I am. Aren't I clever to be using this shipping container?"

The house's call for attention matched Fergus, who was standing in front of the bus, greeting us, dressed not in overalls but in a gray double-breasted suit.

"Welcome to my farm," he said, fanning out an arm to show off his land. "Or, should I say, my workshop—my sanctuary. I'm . . . pleased to have you here."

To other people, Fergus probably did seem pleased, but I knew him better than that. I could tell he was annoyed that part of his "prize" was hosting a field trip, and he'd much rather be sitting on his couch—or grabbing coffee with my mom—instead of having a bunch of snotty-nosed kids on his property. My hunch was confirmed when a kid mistook Fergus's theatrical unveiling of his property as an arm outstretched for a handshake. Fergus jerked his hand away before the kid could touch it.

"Thank you for having us, Mr. Edwards," Mr. Lewis said. "We are all very excited to be here and see what you have in store for us!" He leaned toward Fergus and whispered, "I, for one, am *especially* excited to hear about this new farming method of yours. What a scientific breakthrough!"

Flattered by Mr. Lewis's praise, Fergus seemed to forget his distaste for children and smiled a warm salesman smile. "Why, thank you! But before we discuss the method, I think we should start with a tour!"

Sam, Tim, and I exchanged eager glances. A tour would be the perfect opportunity to snoop. Not only would it give us an idea of where Fergus had hidden the pump, it would also give us the perfect excuse to slip away and inspect the more suspicious areas—we could just say we "got lost."

Much to our disappointment, the tour lasted a grand total of fifteen minutes and didn't go anywhere near the places that could hide a water pump. Fergus steered us away from the barn. He claimed it was too dangerous for kids. Instead, we toured the area around Fergus's farmhouse, which was separated from the rest of the property by a ring of trees and bushes. Farmers do this to protect the soil and block harsh winds.

The surrounding yard was filled with statues and shrubs trimmed in those fancy corkscrew shapes. It was a garden fit for a palace in Europe, not for a farm on the prairie.

The garden was sectioned off by gravel paths. And at the center was a large gurgling fountain that Fergus claimed he had imported from Italy after his travels. I didn't bother to point out that the fountain looked suspiciously like the one on display in Joe's window two months ago.

Lots of people in the town had gardens and lawns, but they were all marked by dry, yellow patches because there wasn't enough water. Since Fergus's plants were all very green, I knew it had to have something to do with that pump.

As Fergus directed our attention to his exotic plant collection, Mr. Lewis raised his hand, asking just how Fergus got such water-hungry plants to grow in the dry prairie.

"It all comes down to the Ye Olde Jenkins Family Method!" Fergus boasted.

Yeah, and stealing everyone else's water, I wanted to add, but I forced myself to keep quiet.

As we proceeded into the backyard, I finally got a good look at Fergus's house. While the front of the house was concrete, the back of the house was one big window. I could see right inside, into one large room Fergus called the living space. It was surrounded by three staircases, two of which seemed to lead to nowhere.

After our tour of the garden, we all sat down on the driveway (not on the garden pathways or the patio because Fergus didn't want us messing up his stuff).

Mr. Lewis cleared his throat. "Class, now that we've had our tour, Fergus is going to tell us about the Ye Olde Jenkins Family Method, which allowed him to produce a miracle crop against all odds. Let's show him some good listening skills, and please wait until the end for any questions."

A hand shot up. "No, George, please wait until the end. . . . Oh, is it urgent? Bathroom? Oh yes, Mr. Edwards do you mind if we? Perfect. Thank you." Mr. Lewis walked away with George as Fergus cleared his throat and stood at the center of the garden, in front of the fountain.

"Now, kids, before I tell you about the method, I have to ask you some questions. Do you or your parents have lots of empty land being saved for rotating crops? Do you switch between growing wheat and barley when you *really* want to grow canola? If you've said yes to any of these questions, then you *need* to use the Ye Olde Jenkins Family Method. This historical technique, handed down from generation to generation, allowed me to surpass the limits of science to grow barley where nobody else could. Yes! Many people—famous people—told me I was a fool to buy this land, that it was unfarmable. But I didn't listen—

and see what I've done?" He opened his arms wide, then paused as if he was waiting for us to clap. When nothing happened, he continued.

"Look, your teacher told me to tell you the history, the secret behind the Ye Olde Jenkins Family Method—that's YOJFM for short—and those who mocked it. But aren't you sick and tired of hearing from scientists who have never even been on a farm? Me too! That's why I'm not going to bore you with the details. Except I'll tell you this: The Ye Olde Jenkins Family Method is the way of ensuring that your crops will be safe from any drought, any flood, any rainfall, any excessive snow, early frost, late winter, early summer, or early spring. It makes your crops more fertile, which means they grow more. You don't even have to seed your crops if you do it correctly."

"Yeah, you just have to steal the town's water," I whispered to Sam, nudging him with my elbow. He pushed back, smiled, and pointed to a gap between the trees where, if you squinted, you could catch a glimpse of the barn. He raised his eyebrows. I turned around and nudged Tim's knee, pointing at the same gap. He nodded. We knew where we were going to go.

I looked for a way to leave without being seen. If we were sitting near the flowers and shrubs, we might have been able to shift toward the rosebushes, then run. But the gravel paths provided no cover. We simply couldn't get away. So we were forced to listen to more of Fergus's "lesson."

"You might be thinking, 'Fergus, look, I'd love to hire you, but I'm a kid and I don't have a farm!' What you don't understand is that I am more than just a farmer. Farming is like life: It gives you experience managing tasks, doing hard work, and growing a backbone. On top of my years of experience as a farmer, I am an accomplished businessman with my own chain of home-brewed sodas, a candy shop, and a DIY mechanics shop. Trust me. Whatever you're doing, I have the experience you need. Any questions?" His triumphant smile grew as hands shot into the air.

"Yes? Guy in the shirt?"

"Where is the candy shop?" Jimmy always cuts right to the chase.

"Um . . . it's in the works. Any other questions? Yes, you. One with the glasses."

"Can I have a soda?"

"No, the sodas aren't for sale. They are being patented. Any questions that are not about the candy shop or sodas?" Half the hands went down. "All right, great. Cutting to the good stuff here. You, tall guy with the hair."

"What's a patent?"

Fergus sighed. "It's a grown-up thing. Anything else? You, other one with the glasses."

"What is the method?" Tim's question caused lots of nods in the group.

"Yeah!" Sam and I mumbled. "What is it?"

"It's the most effective tool for growing. It's the way of ensuring that your crops are safe from any drought, any flood, any rainfall, any excessive snow, early frost, late winter, early summer, or early spring. The best part is, it's ninety-nine percent effective! Trust me: I've never told a lie in my life. Ask anyone around here!" Sam and I held back a laugh at that last part.

"No, but you already said that!" Tim said. "What do you do exactly?"

"W—well," Fergus stammered, "th—that's patented! Next question, yes, you again, tall guy."

"What's a patent?"

Fergus's whole face turned red, as red as the steel balcony. "I already explained that, young man. Any *real* questions? None? All right, it looks like your teacher is coming back."

Fergus turned away from the crowd, ignoring my raised hand. I wanted to catch him in a lie. I wanted to ask why the Jenkins family didn't use this "method" back when they owned the farm. Luckily for Fergus, the last of the Jenkins family had died, so we couldn't ask them.

But we knew the reason. There was no Jenkins method. There was just the Fergus method—stealing the water from the river to make his crops grow.

Mr. Lewis returned with a smile on his face. "Were they good listeners?"

Fergus, already heading back to his house, nodded rapidly, "Great kids, Mr. Lewis."

"Wonderful! I'm sure you gave them a lot to write about!" Mr. Lewis glanced down at his watch. Even though the field trip was supposed to take up the entire afternoon—we'd even switched classes and had English in the morning—it had taken only forty-five minutes.

"We are going to eat our snacks now. Then would it perhaps be possible to see the miracle crop?" Mr. Lewis's eyes glistened with excitement.

"No. It's been harvested." Fergus's sharp response seemed to surprise Mr. Lewis.

It surprised me, too. The crop was there when we had searched for the pump. Why would Fergus have harvested it?

"Well, the bus won't arrive for another hour. Class, after we have our snacks, you can use this extra time to polish up your notes. Mr. Edwards, you don't mind if the kids spread out a bit, do you?"

Fergus shot Mr. Lewis a look that said "I most definitely *do* mind," but kids had already started roaming through the garden. With a sigh of resignation, Fergus said, "Sure. Just make sure they stay out of the plants."

Sam, Tim, and I watched as Fergus walked to the farmhouse, taking care not to scuff his newly polished cowboy boots. Once the door closed behind him, the rest of the class burst into action, skipping off in every direction.

"Stay close enough to hear the bus, everyone! We will honk once to tell you when to pack up!" Mr. Lewis called, chasing after a group that was getting a bit *too* close to the exotic plants.

Tim, Sam, and I locked eyes and smiled. Without saying a word, we rushed off to the gap in the trees. It was time to snoop.

25
THE GREAT SNOOP

"Do you think it's safe to go in there?" Tim whispered. We had made it to the barn without being seen. But we stopped when we saw the roof and its serious tilt.

People from the city—or people who've never seen barns before—have a certain mental image of a barn. They think of a big red thing with freshly painted white trim and friendly animals—like Old MacDonald's Farm.

I'm not going to lie to you—there are some farms that have those nice barns, but usually they are meant for tourists to visit and pet cute baby animals and "feel in touch with nature." Most barns have flaking paint (if any); old, creaking wood; and (whether they have animals inside or not) a peculiar stinky smell that takes some getting used to. Also, the animals bite. That being said, the barn on Fergus's farm made the average barn look like a five-star resort.

The Jenkins family had owned the land for centuries, and over the years, the once glorious barn had started to lean to the left. The wood was weathered and gray, and the roof was covered in generations of birds' nests. Several old, rusted vehicles stood guard around the barn door. Their broken windshields and missing headlights made them seem hollow, like skulls. I shivered involuntarily as we crept past them.

"Whoa, that's a Jeep CJ-8. Those are super rare!" Sam said, pointing at an almost unrecognizable piece of metal with a tree growing through the middle. Tim shushed him. Once a hall monitor, always a hall monitor.

The three of us pushed hard against the barn door. Barn doors are made of solid wood and are usually *super* heavy, so we were surprised when this one swung open easily, tossing us onto the dusty floor.

"Whoa," I said as I stood and brushed myself off. If the outside of the barn was a car graveyard, then the inside was a museum.

The barn was huge, and rusty old tools covered every surface. It was obvious that nobody had gotten rid of anything from this farm. Ever. Not a paint can. Not a nail. A diligent farmer—I'm betting not Uncle Fergus—had organized everything. Hundreds of tin cans lined one wall. At least thirty milk pails stood against another. There were old wooden barrels, splintered crates, muddy tires, and dried-out logs. In the center of the barn, about twenty large objects were hidden beneath decayed canvas tarps and plastic sheets.

"Jemma would love this place." Sam couldn't believe what he was seeing. Tim and I nodded.

Journal, I hate to say this, but as I took in more of the barn, I realized that it wasn't just a museum. It was a zoo. A spider zoo. Every tool, every trinket, every bolt was draped with elaborate spider webs. The webs seemed abandoned, but when I looked just slightly closer, I noticed little brown specks lurking in the depths of the webs—spiders!—waiting to catch their prey. I hate spiders. The only good thing about them is they are food for frogs.

"All right, everyone, let's find this pump. Quickly," I whispered. Sam closed the door, and we began to wander through the maze of objects.

The entry to the barn was clearly meant for small, easy-to-grab things, like pipes or hammers or other hand tools, but, as we got deeper in, the objects became bigger and less familiar.

"Guys, check this one out!" Tim had wandered ahead of us and was staring at something at least a foot taller than him, hidden under a plastic sheet. "Could this be it?"

"Let's see!" Before we could stop him, Sam whipped the sheet off the machine, sending dust and who knows how many spiders flying into the darkness. We all leaped back. The thing underneath the sheet looked like an item from a horror movie. It was an ancient saw with razor-sharp teeth set into a dented metal frame. It had probably been used to cut logs, and it had to be over a hundred years old.

"Well, that's not a pump." Tim coughed from the dust that Sam had let fly.

I grabbed the sheet and tossed it back over the machine. "We don't want anyone to know we've been here." The cover was crooked, but I didn't think anyone would notice. Not in this mess.

"Let's get organized," I said. "No more removing sheets. We will have to peek under them."

We started at the left and circled the barn clockwise. We moved fast. Time was short, and there was so much here to search under. Even though we had started off trying to be as quiet as possible, as our mission progressed, we got more comfortable and started to speak in our normal voices. After all, the class was pretty far away. Plus, whispering too much hurts your throat.

"I think I—oh wait, that's an old trailer."

"Whoa, look at this old gas thingy!"

"Sorry for disturbing your home, Mr. Spider. Please don't eat me."

"Hannah, maybe this is—no, that's not a pump—what *is* this contraption?"

We rallied back and forth until we came full circle and returned to the barn door, tired, defeated, and covered in a century of dust and grime. We had found antique plows and broken-down threshers. Mowers and ladders. Oil cans and hoses. We had even found a wooden wagon, complete with wooden wheels.

But we hadn't found the pump.

"It's not here," Sam said. "Fergus must be hiding it someplace else." He opened the door to leave, and I gave the barn one last look. And that's when I noticed it. Next to the door on the right, there was—nothing. A completely clean space. Not a cobweb. Not a speck of dirt.

"Sam, Tim, look!" I shouted, running to the empty space.

"Hannah, there's nothing there." Sam put his hand on my shoulder. "We'd better go. We don't want to miss the bus."

"Don't you see—that's the point! Look at this barn. Everything is covered in mud and slime! But this one spot is perfectly clean. Something *was* here—but it's been moved."

"Hannah is right!" Tim pointed to some marks on the floor. "I think that's oil."

"The pump must have been here," I said. "But where is—"

Before I finished my question, I knew the answer.

"It's back in the field," I said. "That's why Fergus didn't want the class to look at his crop."

"Who's there?" Fergus's voice, close by and angry, surprised us. We dashed to the largest machine—an old tractor—and hid underneath the canvas that covered it.

We held our breath. At first the barn was silent. Then we heard slow, heavy footsteps.

Thunk. Thunk. Thunk.

He was walking through the barn at an agonizingly slow pace. Who walks like that? My heart started to race. Even with all the adventure—even with our discovery—I was starting to feel like I do in class. Like sitting still was unbearable. I tried to distract myself by listing frog names in my head.

The footsteps stopped in front of us. I could see the shine of his too-clean cowboy boots at the edge of the canvas cover.

He mumbled under his breath, "There is no ghost."

WHOOSH! One of the tarps slipped off a machine. I knew which one—the old saw that I had tried to cover.

"There is no ghost!" Fergus said it louder this time. "You're not scaring me." His voice trembled. "Stop sneaking around and face me man-to-man!"

We froze. We tried not to move. To breathe. To blink. The barn roof creaked. Something skittered away to a far corner.

"There's no ghost. I know someone is here." Fergus's voice sounded strong again. "Are you afraid to come out? Worried you'll end up at the bottom of a well, too?"

I gasped.

Sam's eyes widened.

That was as good as a confession.

"Murderer," I wanted to yell. But if I did, I knew I'd be shipped out to spa school immediately and never have a chance to find the pump and prove what Fergus had done.

We heard the bus honk, but we couldn't leave with Fergus standing there.

My pulse began to pound, but then Fergus sighed and stomped away. "Better go wave goodbye to the brats." He slammed the barn door shut behind him.

We gave him a few seconds, then rushed to the door and peeked out. No Fergus.

We ran for the bus, crouching low in case he was still nearby.

"Hannah, Tim, Sam, there you are!" Mr. Lewis spotted us as we emerged from the shrubbery. "I was doing a final head count and realized you were missing. You're covered in dirt. What did you get up to?" I opened my mouth to answer, but the bus honked again. "Never mind. Our bus driver is on a strict schedule, so we'd better get going."

Everybody else was already seated. Their wide-eyed gazes suggested that we really were filthy. There were no seats left where we could sit together, so Sam joined his soccer buddies, Tim sat next to Mr. Lewis, and I sat next to Mary, who pushed herself up against the wall of the bus to avoid touching me.

Worried you'll end up at the bottom of a well, too? Fergus's words spun in my brain as the bus pulled away.

I will not let him get away with this, Dad, I thought. *I will find that pump, and everyone will know what he did to you. I promise.*

26
THE PUMP

Dear Journal,

On Thursday night, three days after our class trip to Fergus's farm, the enemy was close. Frighteningly close. So close that I could smell the sickly scent of the "special" mushroom casserole he made for dinner. A casserole filled with rubbery chunks of something that may have once resembled mushrooms but had long since been robbed of their texture and flavor. A casserole that was such a unique shade, you couldn't tell if it was brown or gray or green. I reluctantly gulped down this half-baked sludge, pasting a smile on my face and—I shudder to even write this—asking for seconds. This fantastic acting performance was necessary to convince Fergus and my mother that nothing was wrong. When asked about the spa school, I showed—dare I say it—enthusiasm.

"Well, I'm sure Mom told you that when she first described the retreat, I was hesitant. But then I realized it could be fun. Sam was even jealous that I'd get a vacation during school!" That's what I told Fergus. An obvious lie. I would never say anything like that, and when I told Sam about spa school, he had reacted with shock, offering to kidnap me so I could avoid exile. Nevertheless, the lie was necessary to convince Fergus, the casserole-creating criminal, that I would be out of his hair soon.

"That's so great to hear, Hannah! Yes, it will be fun. This place is a state-of-the-art facility, and I don't even want to tell you the amount of favors I had to wrangle. But that should tell you how exclusive the place is. Trust me, you'll never want to leave. More wine?" he asked my mom, who seemed to be relieved that I was no longer rebelling against the retreat and that I was being nice to Fergus.

"Well, if it looks half as good as the brochure, then I'm sure you're right!" I'd taken the brochure up to my room earlier to study. Judging from the photos, students were issued cream, beige, or tan linen uniforms. I guess the people who ran the place were allergic to color. Half the kids in the pictures had the same forced smile as blond-haired frog boy, and the other half had looks not of inner peace but more like complete and total surrender. If I actually went to the retreat, I'm sure I'd be itching to get out by the end of day one. Luckily, I was never heading anywhere near that khaki-clad cult. Sam and I had a plan. It started with sneaking back to the place where we had found Dad's hat. We tried to go back earlier in the week, but Sam had soccer practice, so we had to wait till Friday. Journal, I am very nervous. Practically a whole week has gone by. I hope we're not too late.

"I'm going up to start packing! Thanks for dinner, Uncle Fergus!" I was glad that he didn't respond. Every time he spoke, I wanted to yell, "I KNOW WHAT YOU DID!" I had to focus. To remind myself that we were finally getting close enough to catch him. I rinsed my dishes, put them in the dishwasher, and skipped away. Fergus and Mom exchanged approving looks. To them, the retreat was already doing me a world of good. Little did they know, I was going upstairs to pack for a very different type of trip.

Stay tuned. . . .

Journal, on my way to meet Sam this afternoon, everything hit me all at once. I thought I was finally coming to accept that Dad was dead—until I went into the garage this morning to get my bike and I saw my dad's. I remembered how, when I last grabbed my bike, I'd reminded myself to fill up the tires so it would be ready when he got back. But when I saw his bike today, I realized there was no more "when he comes back." The bike would stay like that forever. It would just rust and gather dust. Maybe it would become a monument that future archaeologists could investigate. They might put a sign beside it:

> DEAD DAD'S BIKE, CIRCA TWENTY-FIRST CENTURY—ORIGINS UNKNOWN

My dad was gone, and the bike was still here—a reminder of all the good times we'd had. A reminder that they would never happen again.

I kicked the bike. It fell over with a clatter. And then I felt terrible. Because it wasn't the bike's fault that my dad was gone.

I spun the front wheel, and it wobbled on its axis. The spokes must have been twisted during my temper tantrum. Fixing the wheel could be expensive, and it's not like Mom will pay to fix it once she realizes that Dad's dead. The bike will be broken forever.

There, I said it. I sat down on the garage floor, trying to push the spokes back into place, knowing that some things can't be fixed so easily. I started to cry.

A beeping sound from my watch reminded me that I had to meet Sam. So I dusted myself off, wiped away my tears, and hopped on my bike.

When I arrived at the Riverway Walk, Sam was standing beside his bike, casually drinking from his water bottle. If it wasn't for the redness in his face, you might have thought that he'd been waiting for hours. He leaped onto his bike, and we were off. Our tires kicked up a cloud of dust and gravel, and I imagined it was so thick, hikers could only see a giant storm cloud approaching them, not two kids riding bikes. We were going so fast, we almost missed the single-track path, which was becoming more and more hidden under the tall grass and falling leaves. Sam beat me to the trail, triumphantly imitating a trumpet noise. I didn't mind being beaten. My mind was focused on the pump.

As we climbed the trail and reached the plateau, I gazed out at the now familiar view of Fergus's farm—and my breath caught.

"Look!" I yelled, and pointed ahead.

I could see it. It was mostly hidden behind the silo, but the pump was there.

My heart hammered as we raced to the aspen grove and stashed our bikes. We snuck over the barbed wire fence, walked around to the back of the silo—and saw the monstrous machine up close.

The entire machine was supported by a green base, balanced on two huge, chunky wheels. **TREASURE HUNTERS LIMITED EDITION WATER PUMP** was etched on its side. Its engine was out in the open, reminding me of the anatomy diagrams on the wall in the nurse's office. Two long, yellow tubes stretched from the machine—one connected to the silo and the other disappeared into a deep, dark hole.

Sam frowned and pointed to a smaller hole with bricks around it. "I bet that was the original Jenkins well. But this enormous hole with the pump looks new. Like Fergus had it dug."

If we had walked around the silo the first time we were here, Sam and I would have seen the holes. But the pesticide warning had frightened us off. Probably just as Fergus had intended. Scare away anyone who got too close.

I stared down into the well. My heart felt heavy, then light, like something that was holding it in place had been lifted, causing it to sink farther and farther into my chest.

What if my dad's body was down there?

What did he feel when he hit bottom? Did he suffer?

Tears stung my eyes.

Then I thought about the ghost. What did *that* feel like—turning into a ghost? Did it happen right away, here in this cold, dark, wet hole? Did he realize quickly that he was dead? Was he afraid? Could he feel anything at all?

How could I be a physical body lifting bales of hay and wiping sweat from my brow one minute and a filmy creature the next? And why didn't my brother—my own brother—try to save me? I imagined my dad asking himself these questions.

"Hannah?" Sam put a hand on my shoulder, but he didn't say anything else. I glanced up from the hole and tried to shake off the weight of these feelings. I couldn't let them overwhelm me. There was too much to do—I needed to show everyone the truth.

"Well, this is it." I wanted to sound professional, but my voice cracked.

"Should we take a picture to show everybody?" Sam asked.

I shook my head. A picture wouldn't be good enough. They might not believe it. Pictures can be made up or edited. People had to see this with their own eyes. "They need to be here," I said. "We just . . ." I kicked at the grass at the edge of the hole. "We just need to figure out how to get them to come. I don't think my mom will believe any more of my stories. Especially since she didn't believe me before, even after I showed her the hat."

I tried to come up with an idea, but I couldn't stop thinking about what Fergus had done to my dad. I don't have a brother, but Sam is like a brother to me. If he ever fell, I'd do everything I could to help him. I couldn't just watch him drown.

I wished I could time-travel back and stop Fergus. Or time-travel back to last night and throw the mushy mushroom concoction in his face. How could he sit there at our dinner table every night, in my father's seat, and say he was trying to help us? What kind of monster could do that?

I shook my head. "I don't know what we should do," I said.

"I do," Sam said. "I know exactly what we should do." His eyes twinkled with mischief. "Remember the Frog Apocalypse?"

27
PLAN F

"Remember the frog invasion? Remember how much it wigged everyone out?" Sam said as we headed for our bikes. "We just gotta create the Return of the Frog Apocalypse. That will get them all down here." It was funny to see Sam rub his hands together gleefully.

Both of us were too young to remember the original Frog Apocalypse, which was seven years ago. But everyone in town still talks about it. And people have articles about it from the *Riverway Rooster* taped to their walls. Even my dad saved one. Here it is:

> **Ribbiting Riverway:**
> **Frog-Horror Invades Small Town**
>
> Ever since the world began, we have been afraid of its end. Some say that the world will go out with a bang. Others say it will go out with a whimper. In Riverway, we are the first to know that the world will end with a *ribbit*.

As the result of what some are calling an "ecological disaster," Riverway was invaded by hundreds of frogs over the past week. Local scientists claim that the low river levels are to blame for these traveling frogs. Frogs are dependent on the surrounding marshlands to survive, and the decrease in the river has dried up the wetlands, forcing the frogs to seek out water. Unfortunately for the townsfolk, these new water sources include the local water park, the town's water fountain, and, in some cases, individual homes.

Unsurprisingly, the sudden appearance of the frogs, especially in toilets, has caused considerable concern. Some parents are worried about the frogs spreading disease. Others—like Jemma, the owner of Jemma's Gems: Rare Antiques and Toys—fear that the frogs are an omen of bad times to come: "Frogs are an ancient sign of witchcraft. Say what you want, but I'm warning you—this whole thing reeks of supernatural danger."

The town council has announced that they will be holding an emergency meeting in the Riverway High School gym at 6:00 p.m. tonight. Until the meeting, they urge the townspeople not to panic; there is no need to riot over *ribbiting*!

Of course, there was no way the two of us could realistically re-create the full scale of the disaster. After all, most of the frogs had been gathered up by local conservationists and shipped to healthier wetlands. There's only one decent marsh now with any frogs left. I went over all this with Sam.

"But we don't need to re-create the whole thing. We just need them to *think* it's happening again," Sam said as we got onto our bikes.

"How are we going to do that?" The part of my brain responsible for planning felt like it was on pause. Like there was a weight sitting on it, preventing it from moving. Luckily, Sam's brain was supercharged right now.

"Well, first we've got to choose some adults to help out. Rick, obviously, but then a couple of witnesses, too. And then . . ." Sam told me the plan.

Maybe grief was making me desperate. Maybe I was being too hopeful. But it sounded like it could really work.

Journal, I know, you want to know the plan. But I can't risk writing it down—just in case someone, meaning Fergus, comes upstairs to snoop. I have to be very cautious around him.

To prepare for our plan, we made a quick detour to the last remaining marsh. It was near the end of the Riverway Walk. In one area, the creek (that used to be a river) becomes very wide, shallow, and slow, creating the perfect environment for marsh grasses and frogs.

Sam and I hid our bikes in the bushes just off the path and walked down to the marsh, our feet sinking slightly into the mud. A red-and-black bird cried out as we arrived, and something splashed in the water. I leaned forward to get a closer look. Even in the murky creek, I recognized the familiar brown and green spots of an American bullfrog. Sam and I smiled at each other.

"So, you're the frog expert. What do we need to catch these bad boys?" Sam asked.

"Well, first we need some nets. Like the type we use to catch minnows. And then a bucket with some water and a cover with lots of airholes. And rubber gloves." If you're ever going to pick up a frog, it is super important that you wear rubber gloves, not for your protection but for theirs: Frogs breathe through their skin, so your bare hands can hurt them.

"I think I have all that in my garage. Anything else?"

"We should probably get them some food. Like bugs. Joe sells bait now. Maybe he'll have some."

Sam grimaced. He doesn't like bugs. He claims it's because they can carry diseases, but I know it's because he fell on a red ant hill in first grade and never recovered from it. "You're on bug duty," he said.

"No way! Everybody talks to everybody in this town. Fergus will find out. He already knows I'm onto him. Plus,

I'm supposed to be going to spa school on Monday. Why would I be buying fishing bait? The bugs are your job." I felt a bit bad making Sam get the bugs, but I couldn't risk getting caught.

"Fine, but you'll owe me one. A giant one." Sam shuddered. "Let's roll."

We spent the rest of the afternoon gathering supplies. We agreed to meet at dawn to capture enough frogs for the plan to work. As we whipped through town on our bikes, for a brief moment, life felt normal. Exciting, but normal. The two of us, on our bikes, having fun. The way it should be.

But when I got home, "normal" slipped away. On the staircase post, where Dad usually hung his hat, was Fergus's newer, far shinier one. I glanced into the kitchen, dreading the sight of him standing by the stove, but he was out back, grilling (or burning) dinner. My mom was standing beside him, chatting casually, her hands occasionally smoothing out the wrinkles in her jeans. It was the image of a perfect family—a happy couple having a late-season barbecue for their kid. But it was all wrong. My dad should have been there. Not this criminal.

I rushed upstairs to write this entry. I'll paste on a happy face at dinner tonight. I'll eat the overcooked hot dogs. And I might actually enjoy them. Not because I like the taste of charcoal. It's because I know if tomorrow goes according to plan, I'll never have to eat Fergus's cooking again. Tomorrow, everyone will finally know that Fergus is a fraud. And they'll know for certain that my dad is gone. Forever. I hate saying that. I hate writing that. But it's true. The pump proved it. Whoever said victory is sweet is wrong. Some victories are overcooked and bitter.

My mom just yelled out that dinner is ready. Wish me luck, Journal.

28
THE FROG APOCALYPSE

"Deep breath," I told myself as I stepped into Jemma's shop. The place seemed even more cluttered than the last time I'd been there. The board-game table was now a great leaning tower, with about a dozen games stacked on top of each other. Four mugs balanced precariously on an arm of the couch. I stood awkwardly in the middle of the room, afraid that the smallest movement would cause everything to come tumbling down.

"Hello?" I called out. My lunch box vibrated as one of its three new inhabitants jumped against the metal side. I hoped they were all right. Sam and I had punched some holes in the box to make sure they had enough air.

"I'll be with you in a moment!" Jemma's voice drifted out from the back room, also known as the kitchen. She sounded oddly sweet. I guess she was up to her third cup of coffee because two-cup Jemma was anything but sweet.

My heart pounded. Jemma's store was my first stop. Then I'd have to round up Joe and Rick. If Jemma didn't believe my story, the mission was doomed. And I'd never done well in drama class—what if she saw through my act?

No, that's just me overthinking things, I told myself. *You don't have to say much. The frogs will speak for themselves.* I started to peek inside the lunch box to make sure they were still okay. That's when disaster struck. As I opened the box, one frog leaped out, making a clean escape. I quickly slammed the lid shut before another one could flee.

For a moment, the frog stood frozen on the coffee table, as if it were dazed. Then it looked up at me defiantly. "*Ribbit.*" Before I could grab it, in one swift movement, it hopped onto the tower of board games. The boxes swayed back and forth. Then *CRASH!* The tower toppled, spraying plastic game pieces everywhere.

"You break it, you buy it!" Jemma stormed out from the back of the shop, still in her nightgown. She had a pricing gun in her right hand, which she held out defensively. Her eyes darted across the shop, searching for the culprit. For one terrifying second, she glared at me, but her gaze softened once she saw that I was too far from the table to be the vandal.

Placing her mug on a cabinet, she stepped toward the mess of board games, sighing. "Guess Joe was right. I was stacking them too high."

As she picked up one of the box covers, the frog leaped out from under it.

Jemma jumped back with a supersonic shriek.

Trembling with fear, the frog bravely launched onto the arm of the couch—and knocked over the four mugs perched there.

"Catch it!" Jemma shouted, waving her arms. "Catch the cursed creature!"

Desperate to keep its freedom (and likely scared by Jemma's screaming), the frog hopped away defiantly, toward a delicate lamp painted with lily pads. It catapulted to the top of the lamp, knocking it over with another loud *CRASH*!

The frog sheepishly looked back at the broken pieces before hopping into a big glass fruit bowl. It huddled at the bottom, trying to hide from Jemma, who was clearly a wild creature best to be avoided.

Well, that was easy, I thought. I held up my lunch box, hoping to show her the other frogs. But Jemma ignored me completely, her glance glued to fruit-bowl frog.

"Shoo! Shoo! Leave!" she yelled.

"What is all that shrieking?" Joe burst in the door. "You're going to scare away—" He abruptly ended his sentence as he took in the chaos—the scattered board games, the splattered mugs, and the shattered lamp. "Wait—what on earth—"

"Look!" Jemma pointed to the frog in the bowl.

"That's what I came here to tell you about!" I jumped in. "There are frogs everywhere near the mouth of the river. See?" I opened my lunch box and showed an incredulous Jemma and Joe the two remaining frogs. I quickly slammed the box shut.

"I came here to warn you so we can do something before they invade the town. You need to get Rick and meet me at the Riverway Walk. I'll lead the way from there. Then you can see for yourselves!"

Joe looked at Jemma, as if he didn't quite believe me. "*Ribbit.*" All eyes shifted to the bowl, but the frog wasn't there.

"*Ribbit,*" it croaked again. It was close. Too close. We looked up and found the frog—dangling right over our heads from a chandelier.

That sealed the deal for Joe. "I suppose there's no real risk in taking a gander."

"No risk? I'd say it's our responsibility to do so!" Jemma stood up, adjusting her nightgown. "I'll get dressed. Then we'll find Rick. And, Hannah?"

"Yes."

"Get that frog out of my shop."

"Joe, can you catch him? I have an important errand to run." I handed him the lunch box. "Show these to Rick in case he needs convincing." I was at the door before he could argue. "Meet you at the south entrance of the path!" I said, then left.

Now all I had to do was convince the most important person of all to come with me—my mom.

29
UNCLE FERGUS
MEETS HIS FORTUNE

"And you're sure that your uncle will be there, too?" Mom said. She was slipping on her coat and looking for her car keys. She was about to go out grocery shopping—I'd caught her just in time.

"Yes! And Sam and Rick and Jemma and Joe! The frogs are back, Mom! You have to come check it out," I told her.

Mom smiled broadly—bigger than I'd seen her smile since Dad had disappeared. "You said there were a million frogs?"

"Maybe even a billion! Come on! I said we'd meet them over by the south entrance. I have to show everyone the way." I tried to make her hurry.

"All right. Let me throw on the right shoes." I tried not to tap my foot as she changed into her hiking boots. "I'm good to go!"

Mom drove us to the south entrance, where Jemma, Joe, and Rick were waiting.

"Where's Fergus?" she asked. She turned her head, looking for him. I told her he'd probably meet us there.

"Well, then we'd better go!" Rick said to me. "Lead the way!"

We all headed down the path Sam and I had taken. I slipped to the back of the group so I could quickly text him:

OMW! Frog Plan in Motion.

Journal, to say I was nervous wouldn't begin to describe what I was feeling. My stomach was churning. My heart was pounding. What would they do when they realized there weren't a million billion frogs at the river's mouth? Maybe I shouldn't have exaggerated so much, but I had to get them there. And worse—what if Fergus had moved the pump since yesterday?

It felt like we were walking in slow motion. How long had we been at it? How much farther did we have to go?

"Did you know we are currently walking on the same path that Wallace "Big Gun" Morrow took during his infamous escape from Riverway?" Rick called out in his tour-guide voice. "After he left this path, he was never seen again." Rick had probably said that a thousand times, but he still said it with awe and enthusiasm. I wondered if he thought Wallace's treasure was really buried somewhere around here.

"Do we have to walk much farther? These shoes were

not designed for this sort of traipsing about." An out-of-breath Jemma leaned against an aspen tree, adjusting the straps of her bright pink sandals. I sympathized with her plight, but I needed her to keep going.

"Well, I'm no geographer," Joe said, "but it does look like the river is ending at that plot of land up ahead." He pointed toward the field that was Fergus's farm.

"Well, that's too far," Jemma complained. "You can tell me all about the frogs."

My stomach clenched. If Jemma turned back, maybe the rest of them would, too. Sam said he was going to release some frogs on this path. Where were they? Had they all hopped away? I bit my lip. Of course, they hopped away! That's what frogs do! They were probably halfway down to the creek by now.

"*Ribbit.*" The sound came from a couple of yards ahead.

"Look!" I called out, rushing past the adults toward the noise. A very dazed frog stood in the middle of the path. The grass rustled, then another joined it.

Yes!

"See? Frogs! There are much more up ahead! Follow me!" I raced in front of everyone, cheering them on.

Five minutes later, as we climbed the hill, we could see the top of the barbed wire fence that marked Fergus's property. Plenty of frogs were hopping around here. *Good work, Sam!*

"Looks like that land is owned—we'd better go ask the owner's permission to use it to descend down to the river." Rick started walking then stopped. "Isn't that Fergus's place? He might even need some help with the frogs."

"There's no time!" I blurted out.

"No time? Hannah, there are certain rules we must follow." Rick placed his hands on his hips. "We can't just go waltzing around on somebody's land. That would make us criminals!" If they only knew the truth—Fergus was the real criminal.

"Look! Over there! There's Sam!" I could see the top of the pump. If I could get them closer to the fence, they'd see it, too.

"Over here! Over here!" Sam waved, and Rick stopped arguing.

"What the heck is that big thing?" Rick scratched his head when we arrived at the fence.

The closer we got, the more monstrous the pump looked. Gears twisted and grinded as the machine gurgled and glugged. It rocked back and forth on its wheels, sending vibrations through the entire ground. **TREASURE HUNTERS LIMITED EDITION WATER PUMP** beamed triumphantly through rust and grease.

"Well, would you look at that." Joe shook his head. "No wonder the little critters are back—this machine must have scared them right out of the ground."

"Did the council approve anything like this?" Mom asked Rick.

"Not to my knowledge." Rick shook his head. "I don't even know what this machine is for. Treasure hunters water pump?" He started to climb over the fence.

"Step away from the machine." A cold, poisonous voice rose up from the hole in the ground. "I can hear you up there. What are you doing on my land?" The same words he had spoken to my dad.

Fergus had placed a ladder in the well. He climbed up and stopped when his head reached the top. His glance traveled from one face to the next. It turned into a death stare when he spotted me.

"What are you all doing here?" he snapped.

"Oh, we were . . . you see, the town has some concerns with . . ." Rick stammered, thrown off by Fergus's coldness, which he usually reserved for kids.

"Frog inspection, sir." Sam spoke with authority.

Rick nodded, regaining his composure. "Yes, it seems that the town may be having an issue with frogs. We were—"

"Well, there are no frogs here, so you might as well move along." Fergus glanced into the hole, getting ready to go back down.

"But there are frogs." Rick pointed to one that had hopped onto his foot. "And it looks like this machine may be the cause of the problem."

Fergus froze. His shoulders tensed.

"I don't see how it could. It's just a standard irrigation machine." His eyes drifted to my mother, and his posture softened. "Barbara, you should have told me you were coming by!" He spoke warmly. "I didn't mean to be so sharp. The machine is just dangerous when it's operating. And when I saw Hannah so close, why, I just got a bit protective."

"I see," Mom replied, clearly not convinced by Fergus's sudden burst of kindness.

"Well, Fergus, you know as well as I that an irrigation machine—especially one of this size—needs to be approved by the town council, especially given your land's unique position directly above the river's spring. Until you've gotten the proper permits, I'm going to have to ask that you cease all work immediately." Rick walked closer to the well. "What exactly are you up to here?"

"Now, Rick, we've known each other how many years? You know how long it takes for the council to approve anything. Can't you cut me some slack?" Fergus pleaded.

"No can do," Rick said.

"Come on, Rick, there's nothing illegal happening here!"

Rick edged closer to the hole, and the rest of us followed him. He ignored Fergus's pleas and inspected the pump, searching for an off switch.

"Rick, come on. Look, I might have cut some corners, but I'm not hurting anybody!"

"Yes, you did," I said. Fergus's head whipped around so he could glare at me.

"Tell them what you did to my father."

Fergus ignored me. "Rick, you're a history buff. You remember the story of Wallace's treasure? What if I told you I think I've found it!"

"Wallace's treasure? People have searched for years, and no one has ever found it." Rick shook his head. "What does this have to do with Andrew?"

"They've been searching in the wrong place." Fergus ignored Rick, too. I could see Mom's jaw clench and the muscles in her face tighten.

"The idea came to me after reading an article about the Oak Island treasure. The pirates set up a whole network of aqueducts and booby traps to keep their treasure safe—people still haven't found it! That gave me an idea: Nobody had ever searched the oldest part of the town—the well on the Jenkins farm. I'll admit, at first it was a breeze. The Jenkinses sold to me without asking any questions. But I hit a small hitch when I realized their well was too shallow. I had to dig a new well, a much deeper one, to reach the aquifer. But now the new well is draining like you wouldn't believe." His gaze turned to the yellow pipe that hung down into the hole. "I'll show it to you."

Fergus lowered himself one rung on the ladder.

"Slow down there, Fergus!" Rick tried to grab Fergus's arm, but it slipped out from between his fingers.

"Tell them about my father!" I yelled.

"What is she talking about, Fergus?" Mom demanded.

"Look, Rick, once we find the treasure, you'll see this was all worthwhile." Fergus moved down the ladder.

"Fergus, how sure are you that there is treasure down there? Even if you're right, you'll only get it after ruining every farm in the county! This plan is absurd!"

"Absurd? More like brilliant," Fergus's voice echoed up from the hole. "You and my brother are both so attached to farming. Time to join the twenty-first century. Most people aren't slogging around in galoshes, slopping pigs anymore. Think of the money! Think of the fame!" He shined a flashlight into the bottom of the hole.

"But what about your prize-winning crop?" Jemma asked. "I thought you liked farming?"

Sam and I couldn't believe what was happening. No one was forcing Fergus to talk about my father. Was our plan going to fail? Was Fergus going to get away with everything?

"That's just a bonus from the excess water," Fergus said. "The real prize is here. Lean over the hole. Look down here. The water is about thigh high, but you'll see something poking out. Something twinkling!"

Rick started to walk to the very edge of the hole.

"Stop!" I yelled. "Don't stand near the edge. That's how my dad died. He fell into this well!"

"Hannah, shut up!" Fergus shouted. "You know, I'm sick and tired of people doubting me. First my brother, then you. There is something down there, and I'm going to find it." He continued to climb down the ladder and arrived at the bottom with a triumphant *splash*. The beam of his flashlight was barely visible in the deep, dark hole.

"Wow. Would you look at that!" Fergus's flashlight bounced off something shiny. "You're about to see *real* history now."

"Fergus. You need to come up and talk to us. This river thing . . . well, it's a real mess. And that ground, it's not stable. And you need to tell us about Andrew. What happened to him, Fergus?" Rick cupped his hands as he shouted into the pit.

Finally! I thought.

"You're just like the rest of them. Can't you see—I'm doing this for you?"

We heard banging. Fergus was trying to dig something out with the back of his flashlight.

CLANG.

"I wouldn't expect any of you to understand—you're too caught up in your own business to think creatively."

CLANG.

"Just a little bit more. It's almost out. Hey, Rick, do you think they can make a statue of me beside Wallace?"

"Climb out, now," Mom said. "And we'll talk about it. Please, Fergus. Come up."

CLANG.

"I've come too far to turn back. I've risked too much. You have no idea what you've put me through."

CLANG.

"The endless hours of working."

CLANG.

"Always the Canola King's invisible little brother."

CLANG.

"Even after he fell, nobody ever checked on me, now did they? No one cared about how I was feeling."

My heart skipped a beat—there, he said it!

"What was that about your brother falling?" I could see Rick was trying to sound calm. "Look, just crawl up the ladder and we can talk."

CLANG.

"I never said anything about him falling."

CLANG.

"Why should I come up there and let you take all the credit for the treasure? For once in my life, I'm going to get what's coming to me."

WHOOSH!

We leaped back as a jet of water sprayed into the air. The ground rumbled underneath us.

"He's broken through to another aquifer!" Rick yelled out. "Everyone, get back! The ground might not be stable."

The *whoosh*ing sound intensified. It seemed to be coming from everywhere at once. Water rushed in to the well and began filling it at a frightening speed.

"Look!" Sam pointed toward the gulch, where the river was filling up. "It's coming back!"

"Fergus? Fergus?" Rick was still standing near the hole, trying to see where Fergus was. "He might be drowning!" Rick shouted. "We need to get help."

Rick took out his phone and started making frantic calls.

Mom looked pale. "I can't believe this is happening." She shook her head.

Jemma and Joe told her everything was going to be all right and to try to stay calm. They wrapped her in a hug. Fergus would be saved, they told her.

But they were wrong.

As the water continued rushing in, the walls of the well collapsed—and we never saw him again.

30
GOOD NIGHT, SWEET JOURNAL

Dear Journal,

    I apologize. It has been a busy few weeks since my last entry. I think I've hesitated to write because I've noticed your pages running out, and I want to make sure that my final entry is perfect. Mr. Roseband (I'll tell you more about him later) told me that perfect is impossible and to try not to worry as much as I do. So here we go.

    The first thing you probably want to know is what happened when the walls of the well collapsed. The search for Fergus was similar to the search for my dad—because they couldn't find Fergus's body. But not as many people brought us casseroles. They weren't all that sad about his death after learning he'd been draining the river for years. The town council meeting on his accident—and the possibility of treasure—was the shortest ever recorded. The council unanimously voted to stop searching for him and to let the river flow.

The second thing you're probably wondering about is if anyone ever found out the truth about my dad. Well, that story is sadder. See, the county police searched Fergus's property, and they found an unmarked grave. They identified the remains as my father's, and the coroner concluded that the cause of death was falling. My mom was devastated, but she held things together. I think she had been expecting something like this for a while.

The few remaining **MISSING** posters of my dad have been taken down. Is it weird to say that I'll miss them?

Because of the news about my dad, I got a week off from school. I could have had longer, but I wanted to get back and see my friends. After the mystery of my dad's disappearance was solved and our farm was no longer at risk, I thought everything would go back to normal.

I was wrong. I'm still distracted, but I'm not hiding it anymore. For example, five minutes into math class, all I could think about was how unbearably slow Ms. Knugen's writing on the board was. I was so busy concentrating on the speed of her writing that I missed another question.

"Hannah?" she said. "Can you convert 23/4 into a mixed fraction?"

"Sorry," I said. "I was distracted, and I don't know how." I expected the class to laugh, to point, to do something, but I couldn't stand lying anymore.

Tim's hand shot into the air. "Don't worry, Hannah. I can explain it!" I knew he wasn't trying to be smarter than me or make me feel bad. He was just happy to help. After class, I rushed to catch up with him and Sam.

"Hey, thanks for helping me out in class. I've been having a hard time concentrating. I mean, school's always been a bit boring, but it's been *way* worse since Dad went missing. I was hoping I'd be able to focus better once we solved the mystery. But I'm still having trouble. My mind drifts—a lot. But I'm going to be working on it. Anyways, I just wanted to let you know." I looked down, feeling oddly embarrassed for having revealed my secret. And worried that Sam and Tim wouldn't want to be friends with me now.

"Don't worry, Hannah. We've got your back," Tim said with a smile.

"Exactly," Sam said. "If you need us, just tell us! We're a team!"

A wave of relief washed over me. I was filled with a sense of determination—it was time to tell Mom. I would do it after school, I decided. But I discovered it was easier to make that decision than to actually do it. I couldn't bear Mom thinking I was a problem. Or worse—a failure.

But the next day, I realized it was too draining to keep the secret from her. I was tired of being on edge all the time.

When I got home from school, I found her sitting at Dad's desk, staring into space.

"Mom? Are you okay?"

She tossed her hair around (like she was dusting out her brain) and gave me a weak attempt at a smile. "Oh yes, honey, just . . . having trouble focusing on this big poster campaign." Her eyes looked a bit red.

"I can relate. Actually, I wanted to talk to you about the same kind of problem I'm having."

"Of course," she said, leaning back in the chair.

"Well, I thought after everything calmed down, I'd be fine in school. But to tell you the truth, I don't think I've ever been able to fully concentrate. Dad's death just made everything come to the surface. And now that we know what happened to him . . . well . . . I still can't pay attention. No matter how hard I try. Everything just goes so slow! Even when it's not slow! And I have to force myself to stay in my seat. I want to get up and move instead of feeling trapped watching teachers write on the board. I didn't say anything about it before because I wanted to be good—to be perfect. But I don't think I can be perfect anymore. But I don't want to go to spa school, and I *definitely* don't want to talk to Ms. Grant."

There it was. People say that when you've told somebody a secret, a weight feels lifted off your back. I felt like my stomach had been emptied—and my brain, too. But it was still a good feeling.

My mom laughed. "That's okay, honey. I understand what you're saying. How about we start with a different guidance counselor in school? I can call tomorrow and see if there's someone appropriate for you to talk to. I know there's another counselor—a Mr. Roseband. And, Hannah, don't worry. I promise I won't listen in."

"Okay, we can try it," I said, telling myself to keep an open mind. As I turned to bring my backpack to my room, Mom called out, "Hannah?"

"Yeah?"

"I really miss him."

I paused. She hadn't talked about Dad since Fergus's accident. At least, not directly. "I miss him, too." As if those words could really say what I wanted to say.

My mom sighed. "Maybe he's still watching over us somehow."

When adults say things like "watching over us," they're not talking about ghosts. They don't have a clue about them. And it's probably not a good idea to try to explain anything about them because they won't believe you. So I buried my urge to talk about Dad's ghost. "I bet he is." That's all I said—and I didn't tell her about my visits to the old mill after Fergus died. I'll get to that in a second, Journal. But first I have to tell you about Mr. Roseband.

I met with him on Thursday. He's probably the furthest thing that you could get from Ms. Grant.

Unlike Ms. Grant's door, Mr. Roseband's was normal. There were no sticky notes, no comics, not even a nameplate. The inside of his office was plain, like my dad's office. There were just a couple of diplomas hanging on the wall, a bookshelf with some unorganized books, and a desk with two chairs: one big and leather, the other smallish and covered with itchy navy cloth. Plus, I could actually breathe in his office. The only smell was the familiar whiff of farm, which seemed to be coming from Mr. Roseband's baseball cap. Even though some people might find this adult approach scarier, I liked it. Mr. Roseband was very straightforward. Dad once told me never to trust somebody who is overly enthusiastic because that usually means they are trying to sell you something. Looking at Mr. Roseband's worn-out shirt and faded cap, I was pretty sure he couldn't sell me anything if he tried.

Mr. Roseband rested his chin on his thumb, smiled, and began to speak in a strong, warm voice. "I know that you talked to Ms. Grant before. Your mom said that you didn't like her. Do you mind me asking why?"

I looked at him suspiciously.

"Trust me. I'm not going to tell her or anybody else about anything you say in this office. I just want to make sure I'm as helpful as possible."

"Well . . . I didn't really find that she was taking me seriously."

Mr. Roseband nodded. "Okay. My job is to listen to you without judging if things are 'serious' or 'not serious.' So, what do you want to talk about?"

I paused for a moment, shocked by the question. I hadn't thought that it was my job to talk to him. I thought it was his job to tell me what I was doing wrong. "I don't really know. What am I supposed to talk about?" I asked, and he leaned back, his eyes twinkling.

"The goal behind this session isn't to talk about right and wrong. It's to talk about your problems and try to find some solutions. From the conversation I had with your mother, it sounds like you've had a hard time with your father's death, and, on top of that, you're having some difficulty paying attention in class. Can you give me some specifics about your problems—say, on a scale of one to five, how hard is it to sit still in class?" He smiled again. The smile wasn't syrupy or fake like Ms. Grant's smile. It also wasn't a happy smile like the type you make when you're singing "Happy Birthday." The smile was more like an invitation to start a conversation. It reminded me of how Dad looked when he was trying to figure out who misplaced the canola seed. It said, "Hey, whatever happened, don't worry about it. Let's just get busy and solve the problem."

"Five," I said, and I suddenly felt lighter. "Next question?" I added, leaning back in my chair. The rest of the meeting flew by as Mr. Roseband asked me a series of questions. At the end, he told me they were part of a "diagnostic test."

"This test looks for all kinds of things. It's our way of narrowing down how your brain works and how we can help you. Now, I don't want to speak too soon, but I think there's a high chance that your results will indicate that you're neurodivergent. There are lots of other neurodivergent people in the school. Neurodivergent is a fancy way of saying that your brain works differently than other people's."

"Differently?" I asked.

"Yes. Differently." He nodded. "Not wrong, but differently. Once we get your results back, we'll find the best way to help you."

I nodded. I wasn't sure how I felt about the possibility of being "different," but the fact that Mr. Roseband could offer help (that didn't involve embarrassing chants) was a big relief.

The results of the test will take some time to come back, but meanwhile, Mr. Roseband gave me some cool bonus powers (his words, not mine), like having extra time on assignments. And my teachers are going to let me pace in the back of the classroom when I can't sit still and feel like I'm going to explode if I don't move. (I just have to make sure I don't disturb anyone back there.)

Today is Halloween, and I am supposed to meet Sam and Tim for trick-or-treating. We are doing a group costume: Tim and I are knights, and Sam is a pink dragon (not meant to resemble *anybody* we know). But before I meet them, I have something I need to do.

According to the ghost book, ghosts disappear once they no longer have unfinished business. If that's true, then everyone learning the truth about Fergus should have allowed my dad's ghost to finally rest in peace. I've been to the Old Grain Mill a few times now, and I haven't seen him—so I think the ghost book must be right.

But the ghost book also says that the barrier between the spirit world and the real world thins on Halloween. Even if my dad is at rest now, there was still a chance I could talk to him one last time.

So here I am, sitting on the floor of the old mill, waiting to see if Dad will appear. I know this sounds strange, but the mill is somehow less scary at night. It's so dark that my mind can't make monsters out of stray shadows.

Okay, my flashlight just moved unexpectedly, making me jump.

"Dad? It's me, Hannah. Are you there?" I called out into the darkness.

No answer.

"Dad, I just wanted to come by and say that I really miss you. And I'm sorry for not believing you when I first saw you. And I'm sorry I didn't pump your bike tires, but I promise I won't let Mom sell your bike. And I hope that, wherever you are, you're happy. And that, one day, I'll see you again."

I waited a few more minutes after that, but I heard only the distant shouts of young kids calling out, "Trick or treat!" I guess that the ghost—my dad—really is at peace. Some part of me feels worse because of it—I didn't get a chance to appreciate him when he was here, even if he wasn't fully here. But then I remembered his distorted face and fading body, and I know that, wherever Dad is, he is happier than when he was trapped here. And I have a feeling that he's never really going to be gone.

Dear Journal, we are finally on your last page. I can't believe our time together is almost done—especially now that you're just starting to feel like an old, trustworthy friend. But it's good to end things on a positive note, and I feel like I can do that now.

After everything that happened—my dad's disappearance, the meetings with Ms. Grant, the ghost, Fergus's death, and the restored river—I finally feel like I have found the key to moving forward. I'm not worried about a life filled with endless casseroles. I'm not worried about something being wrong with me. I don't feel the heavy pressure to be right all the time—nobody is right all the time. When it comes to being perfect, being myself is the perfect thing to do.

Okay—I'm not perfectly happy yet. Maybe I never will be. Maybe there's no such thing as being perfectly happy. But I'm excited. And I'm hopeful. Because, let's face it, there's a lot more in the universe than can be dreamed up in Riverway. And Riverway isn't *that* bad after all.

So, if you're driving south on Highway 1, maybe you should stop here. Come say hi to Sam and Tim and me. You never know what mysteries we might solve together.

Don't Miss Book 2!
HANNAH EDWARDS

Visit Hannah-Edwards.com to learn more!

Acknowledgments

My hope is that *Hannah Edwards* will provide a more nuanced depiction of neurodiversity in children's books, one that focuses less on the rambunctious, distracting hijinks of a poorly disciplined student, and more on the chatty, perfectionistic side of neurodiversity—a side that you may be able to relate to, or at least better understand.

I would like to thank Tracey Hecht for her continual encouragement and inspiration; without her, this novel would not exist. Thank you as well to Susan Lurie for her realistic advice. (You're right: two kids under a sheet probably wouldn't make a convincing ghost.)

I am perpetually grateful to Professor Paul Yachnin for inspiring me to enter into conversations with Shakespeare (even if it feels hard some days).

This book was made possible by the combined moral support of Oscar McCullagh, Thomas Mihelich-Morissette, Remo Gonzales, and Tianna Marinucci—my own Sams and Tims. The writing was fueled by my mother, Lori Hards (an amazing cook), and energized by my father, Eric Hards (an amazing coach). Ian, my brother, stepped in with important truck facts. (Never underestimate the value of a good truck fact.)

Finally, this book was inspired by my lifelong friendships, which will continue to impact me even if they are over for now.

About the Author

Ashley Hards did not have the privilege of growing up in Riverway, the quirky setting of *Hannah Edwards*. Instead, she grew up in the city of Calgary, Canada.

Ashley was declared to be "gifted" at age 8 and was diagnosed with ADHD at age 22. When forced to sit still in class, she found books and writing to be the most engaging subjects, especially Shakespeare. She received both her BA and MA in English Literature from McGill University, where she now teaches writing and continues her research on Shakespeare and ritual.

Always the adrenaline lover, Ashley enjoys skiing, mountain biking, and opera. (Hey, it's exciting.) She spent many weekends driving across Alberta and hanging out at a ski hill near Pincher Creek, and the vision for Riverway developed over many dark, stormy nights (without Wi-Fi or cell signal).

Like Hannah, she enjoys journaling. Unlike Hannah, she has not solved any mysteries (yet). This is her first book.

About Fabled Films & Fabled Films Press

Fabled Films is a publishing and entertainment company that creates original content for young readers and middle-grade audiences. Fabled Films Press combines strong literary properties with high-quality production values to connect books with generations of parents and guardians and their children.

Each property is supported by websites, educator guides, and activities for bookstores, educators, and librarians, as well as videos, social media content, and supplemental entertainment for additional platforms.

Fabled Films Press has published two critically acclaimed children's book series: *Pippa Park* by Erin Yun and *The Nocturnals* by Tracey Hecht.

FABLED FILMS PRESS
NEW YORK CITY

Connect with Fabled Films Press and their characters!

Fabled Films
www.fabledfilms.com
Facebook: @fabled.films.press | Instagram: @fabled.films

Hannah Edwards
www.Hannah-Edwards.com

Pippa Park
www.PippaPark.com

The Nocturnals
www.NocturnalsWorld.com
Facebook and Instagram: @NocturnalsWorld

Great for Ages 9-12!

More Great Books from Fabled Films Press!

"Pippa is a magnetic heroine, funny and good-hearted."
—Booklist

Visit PippaPark.com to read more!